BILLY REID & THE TRACKERS

BILLY REID & THE TRACKERS

The Four Worlds

HAMZA LAWAL

Legend of the Huskahs Publishers

Contents

One

Billy Reid

Once upon a time, there was a boy by the name of Billy Reid who lived in Angel Islington, London. His mother died in childbirth and so he was stuck with his father, who he thought was a rather deadbeat dad. Billy thought his father cared very little for anything in the world outside of watching football — which he enjoyed at a pub or in the living room. He also enjoyed making hysterical international phone calls lasting hours — via WhatsApp. All Billy wanted to do was get a chance to play a video game once in a while, but they only had one TV and it was in the living room. When his father went to work, Billy was at school or had to sleep. It was his elder brother who had 'saved up' to purchase a PlayStation 4 for the duo, but he had been killed just a week after purchasing the video game two years ago. Billy often felt alone and was a scrawny kid who was usually nervous. He spoke very little and now the gloomy winter of London had descended and his father was ever more absent because he had found a love interest — a single mother who had two sons that attended the same school as Billy and didn't like each other much.

"Leave me alone, I'm just trying to go home," said Billy as he tried to run away from the two brothers on his way back from school, but his neck was yanked back from the collar of his shirt. "Mummy said you were gonna be our stepbrother, but we say no thanks, bruv!" the elder of the two brothers teased with an ugly grin on his face. He was very tall for his age. At fourteen years old he was already five feet nine inches, had a face full of pimples and an overgrown curly hair which hung over his forehead like a fringe — hiding his huge forehead which made him look like an alpaca. "I don't want to be your step brother either, Pete," responded Billy, who was quick with his mouth, which often landed him in trouble. He was also two classes below Pete. "Why not? Do you think we no fun?" the younger brother chimed in. A chubby kid, slightly younger than Billy, with a mischievous expression on his face. "I'm just happy being by myself," replied Billy, who then got free from Pete's stranglehold and made a run for it. "G... Get him Segun. What are you waiting for?" stammered Pete angrily and the two brothers began to chase Billy all the way from the end of the canal — where Billy usually used a narrow pedestrian path as a shortcut — to the high street, as onlookers looked on. Billy crossed the road and was only inches away from passing vehicles. A cyclist growled at him for jaywalking.

When Billy finally reached home, the brothers had caught up with him. All three of them — out of breath and heaving.

"What are you boys running from?" asked Billy's father, who had been standing by the door getting ready for one of his graveyard shifts. "They were running after me, Dad!" responded Billy.

"No, no, no. Are you not all brothers? They'll be no more running after eachother."

"Yes, Mr Reid," replied Pete, barging into the house and heading straight for the refrigerator with his shoes on—soiling the carpet. While Segun also found his way into the house and started for the window, picking tiny ceramic figurines of dancing couples and a dainty porcelain ballerina. Billy's father smiled and said, "Boys, don't be picking those things up now. They've been there for ages. Also please, just call me Ade. Pronounced *aah-dei*," spreading his lips apart, revealing a silver tooth as he pronounced his name. "Reid is Billy's mother's family name. After she passed, I thought it'd be a good idea to let Billy have her name."

By the time he had finished speaking, Pete had already eaten all of Billy's sausages and Billy thought about how his life was going to be — stuck with those unruly boys. In the absence of his mother, and his father's nonchalant attitude; Billy and his elder brother were forced to become responsible, grow up fast and take care of themselves. They learnt to cook and clean from an early age, and so Billy regarded the boys as good for nothing.

* * *

Months later, Aunt Sarah and her boys moved into Billy and his father's three-bedroom house. Billy was forced to share his room with Segun since they were about the same age, while Pete had one room all to himself. Billy still felt something turn in his stomach whenever Aunt Sarah touched his mother's figurines—especially the porcelain ballerina. He didn't know why, but he hated it. His life also changed dramatically, as he thought it would. Now he had to share things and often because he was a slow eater, the two brothers would eat everything up before he could. However, although Billy thought his life would be much worse with them moving in, he was beginning to like the brothers and his stepmother wasn't too bad. She was a hairdresser, which meant she was not always at home — a welcome development for Billy. His stepbrother Pete had also made a girlfriend—or so they thought—and was therefore hardly around the house anymore. It was only Segun, the chubby kid, and Billy that were at home after school. Initially, they quarrelled over every little thing, but when no one paid them any heed, they stopped.

***

"So tell us about your new friend," said Aunt Sarah, while serving the boys a breakfast of hash browns and eggs. She had been giving Pete side-looks since he came home from an earlier visit to the park that Saturday morning. "What new friend? And do we have no bacon and sausage?" replied Pete.

"No, we have nothing else because you keep eatin' everything," she responded, her voice trembling slightly.

"Oh, he is a growing boy, hehe," said Mr Ade, but Aunt Sarah wasn't about to let humour dissipate her anger. She had noticed something different about Pete — the staying out late, getting into fights and change in attitude although he had never really been a very well-behaved kid. She reached over to remove the sunglasses he was wearing to see what she suspected was a black eye that he was trying to hide, but he ducked and smacked her hand with the back of his hand. "Are you mad? We have to live with these *bare bukis*—strangers — and now I can't dress the way I want to?" the teenager screamed at his mother and tried to leave the house but bumped into Billy's father, Mr Ade who had barricaded the door. A very brute of a man who had been a construction worker and now worked as a bouncer at a nightclub. "Apologise to your mother, young man!" demanded Mr Ade, but Pete shrugged it off as if he hadn't heard and went straight to the back door, jumping over the fence and leaving the house.

"You know I'm scared that boy might have joined a gang," said Aunt Sarah.

"Do you know anything, you two?" asked Mr Ade, but Billy remembered he wasn't allowed to say anything about a fight that Pete was involved in. He didn't want the conversation to gravitate toward that, so he quietly put his head down. Aunt Sarah's face flushed red in anger as she stood over the two boys. "Aren't you being asked a question? Is he part of a gang?" she asked. Billy finally found his voice but before he could vocalise anything, his stepbrother Segun said, "Pete's been visiting Daddy, innit."

"All the way to Richmond? Why didn't you tell me? You know I don't like you boys going there on your own," replied Aunt Sarah, but Segun was lying to cover for his elder brother. As the conversation went back-and-forth Billy's head felt light and he noticed his mother's porcelain ballerina move slightly. He strained his eyes and observed in disbelief. The porcelain ballerina had moved on its own. So he walked up to the window stool where it was and picked it up. As soon as his finger came in contact with it, an electric surge went through him and he dropped the ballerina on the tiled floor, shattering it to a million pieces.

"What have you done, Billy?" a suddenly berserk Mr Ade questioned, sweating profusely, as if he'd seen a ghost. "It's OK Dad, I'll just glue it," replied Billy. He didn't dare mention what he thought he saw, but that wasn't the first time something strange had happened with the ballerina. When Billy's elder brother was stabbed to death by members of a rival gang, Billy swore he saw the figurine wiggle and vibrate just before the news of his brother's death came.

"It's OK, it's just porcelain," commented Billy's stepmother, Sarah. She didn't know why Mr Ade was stressing over his late wife's furniture so much. Secretly she was pleased as punch that it happened. "Because they are antiques, that's why. They cost money," replied Mr Ade. Billy was relieved his father only valued the figurines because they were antiques. He liked his father's level-headedness and was happy being the only one that experienced 'eerie happenings'. Billy knew you'd need a certain level of rationality to survive in the world, but the mood was about to change to a much sadder note. Aunt Sarah's phone rang for about half a second and she picked it up excitedly, believing it was news about her bookings. "Is that Pete's mother, Sarah?" the voice on the telephone said.

"Yes its me. I'm on the line. What is going on?" she panicked and trembled.

"There has been an incident. Your son is at the hospital. Hello..." At that moment, Aunt Sarah fell on the floor in a panic attack. Mr Ade grabbed the phone from her and spoke with the medics and before long, all four were hospital bound where Pete was—only to receive even more devastating news.

* * *

Over two years had passed since the events of that ill fated Saturday morning, and though the family had tried hard to return things to normal, Aunt Sarah was never really as vibrant as she used to be. Billy's father Mr Ade had become even more absentminded, and bodily absent from the house too. It turned out he wasn't always away from home to be with Aunt Sarah, as Billy thought previously. He was just away somewhere. Segun had lost a lot of weight. While Billy had grown a lot taller. It was his birthday and he could hear the sizzling sounds of sausages on the pan while still laying in bed.

"Wake up Billy, I think mum's done with those sausages," said Segun who suddenly woke up hungry as usual. Billy hadn't received any presents, and he wasn't surprised. He was used to never having any gifts. Though, he was thankful for a birthday cake which his stepmother had bought for him. It would be hours before his father, Mr Ade, returned home — still empty-handed but bearing news.

"Alright, boys, we have decided it'd be best if we moved you away from all this. We are moving to Surrey." Mr Ade said, looking the boys right in their eyes.

"Isn't there where mom is from?" asked Billy.

"That's correct. I'm starting a job there and we can all be off for a fresh start." Segun had nothing to say, but Billy was very excited and couldn't contain his excitement. He jumped up to his feet, grabbed his skateboard and left the house, with Segun following shortly after. "Don't tell anyone at school, Segun."

"I'm not an idiot."

Two

Billy Is Missing

The Last day of school was unexpected for Billy. Much to his chagrin, his stepbrother had told all his friends about leaving the city — who then told others, who told others, who told 'others'. He'd also told them that Billy was very excited. Segun didn't mean any harm, but just couldn't keep his mouth shut as Billy would have hoped. Unfortunately for Billy, some boys had been talking and word spread fast that Billy was 'talking smack' about their 'post code' because he was leaving. Billy always thought himself invisible, but he was suddenly the centre of the wrong type of attention from the wrong type of people. The boys teased him, but what was particularly sinister was when some bullies decided to give Billy a farewell beating.

"Oi, Billy boy!" shouted one bully.

"Don't turn around, Segun, just keep walking," said Billy

to his stepbrother brother silently as they walked home after school. "Are you deaf?" yelled the bully again.

"Run Segun!" screamed Billy. Who ran as quickly as he could. Segun was a little slower. He had hesitated, and the bullies caught up with him. "Why can't you tell your brother to stop? Just want to chat with him. You get me?" said a tall fat bully who couldn't run himself, anyway. The other three bullies carried on running after Billy. There was a loud shriek followed by 'I'm sorry, I'm sorry' — It was Segun. All sorts of thoughts went through Billy's head as he ran around in alleys, trying to avoid the bullies, but he was soon driven into a cul-de-sac.

The alleyway was old, disused, and had cobbled stones all the way to the dead-end where the walls of an old factory stood. There was nowhere else to run to.

"You wasteman. Where you gonna run to now?"

"Please, leave me alone."

"Mandem just want to say goodbye, billy."

"No, you are lying," replied Billy. "Can't we just talk this through?"

"Yeah, we ARE just talkin' innit."

"Lets see if you can find me in here then, losers." A brave Billy said as he squeezed himself through a tiny coal chute on the wall of the old building. It was so tiny that the three boys couldn't go through. "You'll rot in there. We are waiting," One of them yelled as Billy continued to push himself inside. Eventually Billy found himself trapped between two buildings, a lot of rubble, rubbish and a glass window. He picked up a brick and broke the glass. The window led to an underground chamber that formed part of a disused bomb shelter. The air was very stale and Billy struggled to breathe. He saw a door in the corner that was possibly an exit, but was too curious to leave just yet. The basement was cold and clearly hadn't been used in over a hundred years.

* * *

Billy noticed he had turned black like Oliver Twist. He was bathed in coal, cobwebs, and dirt. Inside the basement was a cellar. Looking around, he saw an antique wooden key cabinet. Curious, he tried to open the cellar door. He looked inside the antique key cabinet but none of the keys fit. He moved the key cabinet to the corner, climbed it and was able to reach the coal chute where he came from. He'd hopped he could just find a way back out from there. The bullies must have left by now, he thought but then realised it was blocked. The debris had collapsed further. So it was impossible to go back that way. The door he saw earlier was also locked.

Billy was panicking but luckily found another coal chute that had originally been linked to a building which was partially demolished and another building was built on top of it. What have I got myself into? Poor Billy thought to himself. He was hungry, cold, alone, and afraid and all he had wanted to do was move out of London with his family with no incidents, but he reminded himself that he was now thirteen years old and the days of being afraid were long gone. He was now under Copenhagen Street, somewhere underground. He felt his right pocket and found a small part of the broken ballerina. When the ballerina shattered, the metallic hand was intact, so he kept it and had been moving around with it in his pocket ever since.

He saw another door similar to the one he'd seen earlier,

and instinctively, he turned the doorknob, but it was locked. He inserted the broken off hand of the ballerina and surprisingly, it fit like a glove. Billy opened the door and this time, the room was not dark like the previous one. He saw light from the street, exit signs and a rail track. For a moment, he was happy. He thought he must have been in a London underground station, but there was something off. It seemed like the station was taken out of a train museum from a hundred years ago. He recalled his history teacher had mentioned that there had once been a Royal Mail train that ran across London. So he thought he must have been there, but poor Billy wasn't there. Soon he saw a skeleton on the ground and another on a chair. He screamed at the sight of the skeletons and ran toward the door.

"There is no need to be afraid, young man!" a warm voice came out of nowhere, startling and terrifying him even more. All the blood was drained from his face. He nearly froze, but he gained the courage to say, "Who's there?"

"We've been waiting for you, Billy. I—," the voice said again but was interrupted by someone elese."Oh, stop scaring him. Please, Alfred, and someone turn on the lights," said a woman. She emerged from the shadows wearing a long dress with a bertha neckline. She extended her arm and shook Billy's hands. "Who are you?" asked Billy. He was hoping they could show him a way out. "I am Carla Reid and that's my dog, Alfred." she said.

"Ehem, ehem. I am not a dog. I am a man... I mean, I was a man... I mean — yeah, I'm a dog, but not her dog. I'm my dog," replied Afred as he trotted into the brighter part of the chamber.

"What are you doing down here?" asked Billy. "An' can you show me a way out?"

"Seriously, does it look to you like we ever get outta here?" replied Alfred.

"How can you talk?"

"Don't worry about how I can talk. Get me out of here," replied Alfred, the talking dog.

"I'm trying to find a way out myself," said Billy.

"Well ask your mother," replied Alfred.

"My mother? But my mother is dead."

"Yes, I am dead," said Carla Reid.

"Huh? Does that mean I'm dead, too?"

"No, relax Billy, you are not dead and I'm not a dog," replied Alfred, "we are just stuck here, and you are gonna help us get out — well, except for your mum, she *really* is dead."

"Whaa—" Billy gasped. "I want to go home," he said.

"That's not exactly correct Alfred. You are stuck here, but my son isn't. Follow that door and it will lead you back to the human world."

"O'...O...Okay. Goodbye Carla, Mummy, goodbye Alfred," replied Billy. He turned around and hastily made for the exit in the direction where Carla Reid pointed. It was a door with stairs. Billy sighed in relief. He climbed and climbed disused crumbling staircases and finally saw himself at Old Street station. He was glad he was finally out and back to the real world. It was already 8:00 o'clock at night and he was exhausted. Passersby looked at him funny, as he was covered in coal and dirt. On his way back home, he saw Alfred barking at him and wiggling his tail.

"Alfred, how did you get out?" he asked, but Alfred just stood there panting with his tongue out and a 'woof-woof' here and there. "So you can't talk, Alfred?" Alfred looked sad and lowered his head, acknowledging Billy that he was unable to speak. "Well, come on then, let's go home." Alfred happily followed Billy home.

Meanwhile, Mr Ade and Aunt Sarah had been going crazy trying to find Billy. They'd phoned the school, the hospitals and even the police. While his stepbrother, Segun sat silently believing he had caused him to get shanked somewhere, and that it was his fault but he was too cowardly to say anything.

When Billy returned, he was scolded for staying out late and getting everybody worried. Billy had such a fascinating day that he didn't bother telling anybody what he'd seen or where he'd been. Segun was relieved to see Billy alive and well.

"Where did you get that dog from, Billy?" Asked Mr Ade. He looked so pale in the face. "I found him, Daddy. Can we keep him?"

"He looks very familiar. Hmmm."

Three

The Reid House

"So I haven't been completely honest with you guys. Listen Billy—," said Mr Ade while driving down the motorway. He wanted to say something important, but thought it would be better if he stopped the car. So he slowed down, swerved to the left and indicated that he was about to leave the main road. He parked the car by a cafe off the A3. "Well, it's a good thing you are stopping. We could all do with some refreshments," said Aunt Sarah. "What would you boys like to have?"

"I need to go toilet, still," said Segun. He was tired and upset about leaving London. So he pretended he hadn't heard what his mother had said. Billy stepped out to stretch his legs and Alfred jumped out, too. "Alfred, don't go too far," cried Billy, who was also too concerned about getting Alfred back, that he didn't care replying Aunt Sarah.

"You need to get a leash on that dog," said Aunt Sarah.

"He just won't stay still," replied Billy.

"Where did you find him, anyway? I don't really like that dog. It's almost as if he can hear exactly what people are talking about." Aunt Sarah shook her head, looking at Alfred as he pranced on the grass trying to catch bugs.

"Oh, he's just a dog, Sarah, and I think your mum used to have one just like that, Billy. Billy? Where's Billy?" Mr Ade asked, looking around, remembering the ordeal they went through when Billy went missing the previous week.

"He's over there near the cafe — trying to get Alfred. Oh, that dog!" Aunt Sarah lamented while motioning for Billy to hurry.

They were all sat at a table in the nice cosy cafe called Nice-Bites, except for Segun, who had only just barged in. He sat next to Billy and ordered the second largest meal, after Mr Ade. That was something they both had in common—large plates with lots of meat. Another common thing they had was 'itis', as Billy would say — a slang he had learned from a TV program which means a feeling of laziness after a meal. How is his daddy going to drive all the way now? He thought.

"What did you want to say earlier, Dad?" he asked, while enjoying a plate of fish and chips. "Well, yes, I wanted to say that your grand uncle Campton has just passed and has left his property to you. So you have his house and that's where we are going to li—," before he had finished his sentence everybody gasped in shock. While Mr Ade gave out a little titter. "Like I said, you are going to like it there. Everyone will have their own rooms and maybe we can even have another kid."

"So we are going to live in a manor?" A gleeful Billy asked.

"Well, not exactly a manor, but quite a big house," Mr Ade

responded with a yawn, "... I think we should go before I fall asleep here," he added.

"On a journey somewhere?" asked the nice lady who worked at the cafe.

"Yes, we are moving houses. Can we please have the bill?" replied Aunt Sarah. The kind lady nodded in the affirmative and went over to the cashier. "Don't bother bringing it over hun, I'm coming," Aunt Sarah stood up and noticed Alfred had been sitting under the table. "Move over there, gosh," said Aunt Sarah. "This dog doesn't behave like a normal dog. Maybe try calling him Alfie, 'hidie', since he enjoys hiding around," she snapped. Alfred snarled at her for saying that and moved to the other side of the table. "He's a Labrador. Though I think he might be an American Labrador — because he doesn't have an 'otter tail' and his temperament is slightly different," Mr Ade observed curiously.

"When did you become such a dog expert, honey?" asked Aunt Sarah.

"I actually remember Billy's mother having a dog just like this — I don't remember his name. Oh, but that was so long ago."

"Alright boys, let's go," said Aunt Sarah, who was also visibly happier, though she must have known all about the house, all along. She also didn't want to hear more about what Billy's mother had or didn't have — they were already moving into the house Billy's mother grew up in. Segun was finally showing signs of excitement about the house. He kept looking out the window and pointing at different houses, saying 'it could be like this one or it could look like that one'. The rest of the drive was calm and luckily, Mr Ade didn't fall asleep on the wheel. Thanks to Aunt Sarah and the boys who kept chatting all the way.

When they finally arrived at Stony Oak — a lonely neighbourhood—, they saw the large, red brick Victorian building from a distance. As they got nearer, they noticed a moderately sized garden with overgrown shrubs. Its exterior wasn't very welcoming, but the interior was fabulous. While Aunt Sarah and Mr Ade went about sorting boxes, the boys went exploring the neighbourhood.

*　*　*

The streets were narrow, and the sidewalks — shaded by majestic old trees. The road was like a golden arrow lit by the evening summer sun. The house stood alone in the corner in front of a large forest—only a stone's throw away. The neighbourhood was rather sparsely populated and buses ran only half-hourly. So Mr Ade had to sign the boys up for a school bus to pick them up every morning for school. There was a lone house on the hill, but the other houses were all clustered together except for their new house, which was also a stand-alone.

Billy finally put a leash on Alfred, but he could tell Alfred hated it. The poor dog tried and tried to take it off, but eventually gave in. By then, Billy had hoped and wished that he imagined the whole episode and that Alfred had never talked, but he knew he couldn't convince himself of that. He was certain Alfred could talk, but he couldn't afford to tell anyone such a strange thing.

The house grew smaller and smaller as they walked farther and farther away. It looked exquisite from afar, thought Segun. "So, where were you last week, Billy? You keep saying those 'roadboys' couldn't catch up with you. Are you sure?" Segun inquired, while bouncing his basketball as they explored the new neighbourhood. "Over there, come on, let's go to the house on the hill," said Billy, who trekked faster as he approached the hill, deliberately changing the topic. He tossed a stick for Alfred to fetch and the dog ran fast toward it. "Hey slow down Billy," grumbled Segun, who was growing tired, keeping up with Billy. "Look at the view from here, Segun. You can see our new house completely."

"Oh breathtaking. So where were you when you went missing?" Segun asked again for what seemed the like the umpteenth time.

"Did you just call the kids that were after me roadboys? I thought you wanted to be a roadman too, Segun," Billy laughed loudly, but Segun looked at him with a straight face, demanding an answer. "So?" he asked again.

"Well, I'm not quite sure, Segun," replied Billy. Segun's eyes wandered off and then focused on a spot toward the house on the hill.

"Look over there, Billy. There's a girl."

"Yeah, I saw her," replied Billy.

"Alfred is on their porch," observed Segun. The two boys walked over to the porch of the lone house on the hill. The girl was seated on a mobility scooter, reading a children's encyclopaedia. She had a pair of jeans on and a white blouse, brown hair, and freckles. She waved at them and they waved back. "Alfred, let's go!" shouted Billy.

"Hey, are you moving to the old house down there?" the girl asked with a smile on her face. "Yes we are. I'm Billy and this is my brother, Segun. We are from London." The girl became animated. Full of excitement, she said, "Welcome to Stony Oak. I'm Audrey and I live here. See you around," she said. She manoeuvred her mobility scooter and rolled in an opposite direction. "Can't she walk?" asked Segun.

"Hey, I can hear you. Of course I can walk," she replied as she reached the side of the building and almost disappeared from their view behind a few branches. She used a remote control to open a side door that had been designed for use with a mobility scooter. Just before going in, she turned around and shouted, "Your new house is haunted, you know. Just warning you." Both Billy and Segun looked at each other, slightly bemused, and Segun said, "We'll see!"

* * *

Few days later, summer holidays had ended, and the boys had started in a new school. Billy discovered Audrey was in his class and that she was incredibly clever. She helped him with a math sum and even sat with him at lunch. Segun, who was a class lower than Billy, found the school less accommodating. He missed his elder brother Pete and missed his old school. He had no friends yet and so usually had lunch together with Billy when on break, but one day he had skipped lunch and arrived late but just when he spotted his step brother Billy, he noticed Audrey was just leaving his table, gently wheeling herself away. "What are you, friends now?" he asked.

"Shhh, she can hear you," replied Billy.

"Yes, I can hear you," Audrey responded.

"Oh sorry. Your hearing is crazy, though," a mortified Segun blurted.

"I'm gonna come explore your new house today. Any ghost yet?" Audrey said with a smile on her face, her large blue eyes twinkling with excitement as the light of the sun dispersed under the skin of her face. "No, I have seen nothing, but it is creepy at night," replied Segun.

* * *

That afternoon after school, Audrey arrived, and they began exploring the big old house, but they saw nothing they hadn't seen before. It wasn't until one cold October evening that Billy heard voices coming from downstairs. He knew Aunt Sarah and his father were asleep, so it couldn't have been them. He got out of his bed, slipped in his slippers and looked at his phone to see the time. It was nearly two in the morning. He headed to the stairs, still hearing murmurs and even laughter. As he reached the landing, he heard knocking on the wall. How is that possible? He thought. There was nothing behind that wall, or was there? More voices accompanied the knocking and then singing. Billy realised it was coming from behind an old grandfather clock.

There must be a door that leads to the neighbour's house, he thought — not a big deal. He didn't want to move the clock and risk waking everybody up or accidentally causing it to tumble over down the stairs. He went back to bed, pulled over his duvet and then realised they had no neighbours on the other side of the wall — It was a lone house too just like the one on the hill. He promised himself he'd investigate in the morning. Billy slept like a baby, but Alfred's wet tongue interrupted his snooze, licking his ear. He woke up and saw Segun standing over him, his bedroom door wide open and the light of the sun shining in his eyes.

"You should have seen Alfred. He was so excited about the old grandfather clock on the landing, so dad moved it. You can't believe what we found behind the clock. It's a small room with all these dumb old photos," said Segun. Billy stretched his arms and grabbed Alfred, moving him to the floor, but Alfred pounced on him again. "Alfred, what did I say? No beds! bad dog!" said an irritated Billy.

"Alfred's been hyper all morning..." said Segun. He paused for effect. "... I think he wants you to see the hidden room."

Billy was not sure what he was more surprised about at that moment. That Segun finally called Mr Ade, dad or that there was a hidden room behind the old grandfather clock. With a puzzled look on his face, he stood up and headed to the bathroom to freshen up. Right after, he went straight to the landing and into the room. There were four large photographs on the wall. The room smelt of mould, had spiderwebs everywhere, a table in its centre and four chairs. As Billy examined the table closer, he noticed a planchette covered in dust. He picked it up gently and read a scribble on it that said 'ballerina'. What a curious thing. Why would 'ballerina' be written there? He thought. "What's that?" asked Segun. The question prodded through Billy's deep concentration, making him drop the planchette on the old Victorian rug on the floor. "It's a planchette," replied Aunt Sarah. "The Victorians were obsessed with seances. I think that's what this room was used for—clearly." She stepped into the room, looked around and saw the photographs on the wall, and noticed a light from the ceiling. "Well at least there's a little window up there. Alright, let's close it back up, it's too dusty," she added.

"But we are still exploring," responded Billy and Segun in unison.

"No, everybody out or you are going to catch a cold. And what's with Alfred? Oh, this dog. Why won't he leave this room?" she asked a rhetorical question. Clearly irked by Alfred.

"Come on, Alfred, let's go!" said Billy depressingly. He didn't want to leave, and neither did Alfred. Aunt Sarah closed the door, but she did not move the grandfather clock back to its previous position. So the boys were getting ideas about returning to the room at some point.

Carla Reid observes from a distance...

Four

"Fake Doors?"

"Why didn't you guys call me? It would have been nice to see the opening. You know, the first time the room had been opened in probably like a hundred years," effused Audrey.

"Yeah would have been really nice indeed, Segun," Billy concurred, giving Segun a side-look as if to say: you opened it without me either. "Oh, you guys are gonna gang up against me?" Segun responded, shaking his head, "Alfred wouldn't stop barking at the clock — that's why it was opened." He cranked up the speed of his scooter going downhill from Audrey's house. Seeing as Segun sped up, Audrey also increased the speed of her mobility scooter and followed Segun closely. It was just Billy, who only had his legs to use. "Hey wait up, guys!" he yelled.

At the house, an excited and eager Audrey couldn't wait to see the room. "OK, give me a hand, Segun. Let me get the key. It's on top of the grandfather clock," said Billy.

"I thought we weren't supposed to go in there," responded Segun.

"We are just showing Audrey the room for like a minute," replied Billy but he was actually just as curious and excited about the room as Audrey and in particular Alfred, who was right in front of everyone wagging his tail and salivating as if he's going to be given a stake in there.

As soon as Audrey got into the room, she went straight to the wall and placed her hand on the wallpaper. "It seems there was a door knob here before, and over there too. I think the photographs are placed on top of doors and covered by wallpaper," she theorised, as she observed the room. "Good spot. According to Aunt Sarah, the room was used for seances," said Billy.

"So that's why people say there are ghosts in this house," responded Audrey.

"Who says that? You guys sure are funny believing stuff like that?" guffawed Segun. He shook his head and made his way to the door. "Nothing but dust here," he added, but just before leaving, he saw a small drawer. Curious, he opened it and found a ouija board inside. He turned around and realised Audrey and Billy had been staring at him. "What is that?" they both asked in unison.

"I don't know. It has letters on it," responded Segun.

"It's a ouija board," said Audrey. Alfred wiggled his tail, and his entire body wriggled from side to side. He was so excited. While Billy looked anxious. He remembered his ordeal underground when he disappeared just before they moved to the new house. He thought maybe it would be a good idea to leave the room before anything strange happens again, but Alfred snarled at him for even thinking about that. He also looked at how excited Audrey was and how Segun had suddenly developed a renewed interest in the room, so he stayed put.

"So what's behind the stupid doors, anyway?" asked Segun as he placed the ouija board on the table. "I think they are just fake doors. They were—," replied Audrey.

"I don't think they are fake doors," interjected Billy. At that point, he remembered his otherworldly experience in London and exactly what 'ballerina' scribbled on the planchette meant. He placed the hand of the ballerina inside a curious-looking slot, which was on the side of the planchette and it fit perfectly. He then placed the planchette on the board and no sooner did he do that than the room started vibrating. Billy reached over and grabbed Audrey's hand so she wouldn't fall while Segun steadied Alfred and then the vibration came to an abrupt stop — just as it started.

Eerily, the same strange sounds and songs that Billy heard the other night started coming from behind one of the fake doors. "What is going on?" asked Audrey.

"Look, the man in the picture is s—smiling," stammered Segun, fearfully. The smiling man then stepped out of his picture. He looked at all three of them and said, "You are most welcome to our rather fanciful abode." The man was ghostly and although he was bluish and transparent, it was still possible to see that he was dressed like an upper class Victorian and his face looked friendly. He then began to sing:

"You find so many people are dutiful

But you, you are mostly beautiful

I like the way you run.

You do it like a hun.
I like the way you love.
You do it like a deneuve.
I like the way you dance.
You do it like vance.
You find so many people are ornamental
But you, you are mostly gentle
I love the way you wear your hair,
Spreading your style everywhere.
You're like a style fountain.
Enough zazz for a whole mountain.
You find so many people are downbeat
But you, you are mostly sweet
You're the perfect girl.
Leaving me in such a whirl.
You find so many people are dutiful
But you, you are mostly beautiful
Beautiful, heavenly, and gentle,
Sweet and empyrean too,
Are the qualities of you
You find so many people are ornamental
But you, you are mostly gentle!"

The ghostly man then performed a pirouette. He kept twirling and twirling until he disappeared back into the photograph.
The three of them gasped. What had they just witnessed? Segun
furtively glanced at the picture and saw that it had returned to
its original position. He then scuttled off, opened the door and
ran out of the room, with Alfred right behind him and Audrey
and Billy followed next. All pale in the face with fright but
with a subtle hint of excitement, they gathered their strengths
and returned to the little hidden room. Billy found that the
ballerina's hand had come off the slot in the planchette which
it was lodged in. Segun closed the door behind him and they all
agreed to try again. At that moment, a sound came from downstairs. It was the front door closing. "I think that might be Aunt
Sarah. Please let's keep it down," said Billy. Segun and Audrey
nodded in agreement.

Aunt Sarah glanced at the dining table and saw that the boys hadn't even touched their lunch yet. She looked in to their rooms but there was no sign of them. So she thought they must have gone to Audrey's house from school. She poured herself a glass of wine, sunk into her massage chair and turned up the volume of an episode of her favourite TV programme. Meanwhile, they were actually in the Hidden Room by the landing of the stairs.

"Alright, let's try this again," Said Billy. He inserted the ballerina's hand inside the slot in the planchette and the room vibrated again. This time, the door under the photo of the ghost who had sung earlier opened and Billy's mother stood on the other side.

"Mum?" said Billy. Segun and Audrey looked at each other in disbelief while Alfred trotted through the door, almost galloping. "Yes, my son, come in. It's okay, I won't let anything bad happen to you," replied Billy's mum. Billy reminded himself of his experience in London when the bullies were after him. He recalled how terrified he was and how his mum showed him the exit and how he got home safely. Her words were reassuring, so he glanced at Audrey and Segun and said, "Come on guys, we can trust her. That's my mummy." They carefully walked to the wall, which had now turned into a door, and they went through. The door shut firmly behind them. Aunt Sarah, who had been dozing off on her massage chair, thought she heard something up there. She stood up sleepily and went up to the landing and peered into the room, but she didn't see or hear anything.

* * *

"Oh, finally, we made it back here again. The boy did really well. I can tell you that Carla — he's a clever one," said Alfred.

"Aaaaah!" screamed Audrey in shock.

"You surprised I can talk? I keep telling people I'm not a dog," responded Alfred.

"Oh, you've always been a dirty dog, Alfred," said the ghost from the photograph who had sung earlier. "Alfred was a thug, a larrikin from London who forced children to work for him even after 1833, when child labour had already been regulated," the ghost continued. He did not appear like a ghost anymore. He was solid, had perfectly gelled hair, and spoke in a confusing Victorian style. "Oh please! All factories did that, everyone did that. I was just following orders," replied Alfred. He reached over and grabbed a bottle of champagne. Audrey couldn't take her eyes off him. How is a dog holding a bottle? She thought. "Is that so? And what about the exorbitant rent for the girls at Whitechapel? Still taking orders? And if they couldn't pay?" responded the ghost with a stern look on his face. "Okay, okay, I wasn't exactly a saint," Alfred finally conceded.

"And who are you?" Asked Billy.

"Pardon me, my most respected guest. We have been awaiting you for a very long time. I am Arthur Broadbottom, the Earl of Stony Oak," he said with a bow. Billy looked over at his mother for approval, and she nodded. While Segun thought the ghost's surname would have been funny in a different setting. "What about Alfred?" he asked, still not able to get over a talking dog. "Alfred was ruthless, yes, but he's already paid his dues. Unfortunately, something isn't right. People aren't dying and moving on anymore. He's trapped as a dog — life after life," replied Arthur Broadbottom.

"How is Billy supposed to help you?" asked Audrey.

"Well, yes, Billy is the prophesied one. Though he'll need help," replied Arthur Broadbottom. He bowed at Billy again. Billy's mother, Carla, nodded at Billy to reassure him. "That is why I'm here to help. I chose to return here and wait until Billy is of age," she said, her eyes resting on Billy for a while and then she glanced at Audrey and Segun and continued, "we all have roles to play."

"So how long have you been waiting here, Mr Arthur?" asked Segun.

"Oh, don't worry, time here is not so evanescent as in your world. All three of you must return now, find a book in a chest in the basement; it contains all the information you'll need. The book is called 'The Book of Doors'. You can't miss it."

Arthur Broadbottom transformed into the bluish spectre he was before. It started from his legs, then it went slowly up to his head and he disappeared. As for Billy's mother, she turned into a white light and diffused in the background. "What's happening to me? Aahh Ahh! I can't see myself," shouted Alfred.

"Go now if you want to return to the human world, Alfred!" responded Arthur Broadbottom. Segun ran and opened the door leading to the Hidden Room and Alfred jumped back in. It seemed the ghost-effect had no impact on the three of them except for Alfred.

Five

The Book of Doors

"Okay, that was crazy. Yesterday was definitely the weirdest experience I've ever had," said Segun, still reeling in disbelief. He glanced over at Audrey, who had just arrived at the Reid family home. He didn't even bother asking Billy what he thought because it seemed like that wasn't the first time Billy had seen his dead mother — so he was definitely used to strange things like that, anyway. "I totally agree with you. Couldn't get any sleep last night—and I haven't told my parents. They just wouldn't believe it," replied Audrey. For the first time, Segun noticed a mark on her arm. "What's that?" he asked, pointing at the mark.

"Oh this. It's just a birthmark," said Audrey, pulling her sleeve to cover it. "Where's Billy, anyway? Found the book yet?"

"Billy is in the basement looking for the chest or whatever. I'm keeping a lookout here. You know the parents don't want to see us down there. It's not renovated yet," Segun replied, leaning on the edge of the basement egress window in the garden. The garden had overhanging branches, and over at a corner were a collection of trees and shrubs obscuring a grave monument. Audrey wandered off to explore the garden, and she spotted the tomb stone. "Wow, it says Arthur Broadbottom, 1813 to 1876. This is where he is buried," she observed.

"Creepy, but I like it," replied Segun. Moments later, Billy was done. After rampaging through piles of rubbish, books, and more books inside the chest, he finally found what he was looking for.

"Hey guys, I found the book," yelled Billy from the basement, his voice echoing on the empty walls.

"Roger that. Coming!" replied Segun. He ran to the back door, got into the house from the kitchen, and held the door ajar for Audrey to enter. "Thanks, Segun!" said Audrey. She stepped off her mobility scooter, putting all her weight on one leg while holding up the other leg. "You can walk?" asked Segun.

"Only my right leg works. I can't feel anything on my left. That's why I use a mobility scooter. Help me bring it in, please," she said.

"OK, I got this," replied Segun, who was in a rush to see the Book of Doors, but saw Mr Ade standing in the sitting room instead. Mr Ade was looming over the book, which was placed on the coffee table at the centre of the living room, and Billy; seated at the dining table having lunch. "I see you've found The Book of Doors," said Mr Ade. "Billy's mom was obsessed with that book when we were teenagers. She moved to London with it, too. I don't know how it ended up back here at Uncle Campton's place. Anywho, I'm going to work now," he added, while packing his sandwiches into his small bag. Segun went to have his lunch while Audrey started reading the Book of Doors. "Would you like something to eat Audrey?" asked Aunt Sarah.

"No, not hungry," replied Audrey. She was too eager to open the book. By the time the boys were done with their meals, Audrey had already glanced through the whole book.

"So what's the book about?" asked Billy.

"Well, it's all about this house actually, and how to use those doors in the Hidden Room." Unfortunately, the book was hard to understand because it was just so old and it had strange words the teenagers had never heard of. Strange symbols and even Latin. Billy was sleepy from all the reading Audrey was doing and Segun had sneaked upstairs with Alfred into the Hidden Room. He had tried to do exactly what Billy did the last two times but nothing happened. The room didn't vibrate, the door did not open, and neither did a ghost emerge from one of the photographs on the wall, or so he thought. He slowly crept back down and sat next to Audrey just as she turned to a chapter called 'History of the Doors', which read:

"A long, long time ago, before this our age, primitive man discovered doors that open to other worlds. Therefore, markings were made to indicate all such locations throughout the earth, but in this our age we have put together this house — a technology which by itself is something of a wonder. Under the right conditions, those who are chosen can access the worlds at will. However, care must be taken. Let no one attempt to enter any world without first necessary initiation designed by a teacher as the teacher sees fit. The four doors represent entryways into the four primary worlds most resembling this our beloved world. After passing through a door, the traveller must turn left, never right.

A door will be there and that is how to access the world. A thorough knowledge of the apothegms of each world must be known or a traveller will, without a doubt, be on a road to perdition. Like the physics of this our beloved world that we have all become masters of, {such as gravity}, so too, must a traveller master the physics of the destined world. A balance must be maintained by the chosen ones of every era. Otherwise, the boundaries between the worlds will collapse and the worlds will merge — that must not be allowed to come to pass."

Audrey stopped reading to catch her breath. She glanced at Billy and Segun to see what they thought so far. Segun was half asleep next to Alfred, who was also sleeping, but Billy was listening attentively. Audrey flipped through a few more pages and reached another chapter entitled 'Strange Plants'. By then, Segun had woken up. The boys leaned closer and saw drawings of some plants that they had seen in the garden of the old Victorian house. She flipped through more pages and Segun said, "That's interesting, it's Broadbottom, look!" There was a sketch of Arthur Broadbottom and the other three people in the photographs upstairs. It was under a chapter called 'From the Reid Blood'. "Let's read this chapter," said Audrey.

"Though not all of us that have come together in this, our union are of the Reid bloodline, we however, cannot disregard the efficacy of the bloodline of some among the Reid family in this our craft of thaumaturgy. For in experiments we have seen how ensorcellment harms them very little. They also have faster recovery from all things from worlds beyond this our world—for that reason we theorise, that perhaps it is from whence the bloodline originally emanated."

"Aaargh translation, please," said an upset Segun.

"Its something about how some people can survive better in a different world—maybe like Billy," replied Audrey.

"That could be how I was able to survive in that place in London," said Billy. Audrey nodded and then continued.

"Therefore, we at this moment in time have, after careful deliberation, appointed from among us four teachers. The photographs of the four teachers are placed in front of the doors in the Hidden Room. Essential knowledge of spells must be learned before entry into the worlds, for that is the only way to ensure survival. When ready, a chosen one will be contacted. Such a chosen person has all rights to take with himself or herself apprentices, companions, or friends. To access each world, trials must be completed. The four great teachers are Arthur Broadbottom, Viktor Ripmav, Carla Reid, and Rabeus Farabus. The teacher in charge of door number 1 is Arthur Broadbottom, the Earl of Stony Oak. He teaches basic survival skills necessary to survive in Azrea. The original entryway to Azrea is in the village of Pluckley, but with the technology of this masterful house, one can enter from here. The teacher in charge of —"

Audrey stopped reading and looked up.

"Why did you stop?" asked Segun. Audrey looked upset.

She sighed and said, "well, the pa—" but before she could finish her sentence, Mr Ade interjected,

"The page is missing. That's the most annoying thing about the Book of Doors—so many pages are missing. I think it would have been a great board game. If you turn it over, you'll see. 'It says board game'." He dropped his bag on the floor, removed his shoes, and headed upstairs. Aunt Sarah heard Mr Ade come in, and she realised it was quite late at night. Why didn't he tell Audrey to go home and why didn't he tell the boys to do their homework or to go to bed, she thought. Immediately, she went downstairs and instructed the boys to head to bed. On seeing her, Audrey—whose back was sore from reading in an awkward position for so long — hurriedly made her way out. "Goodnight Mrs Ade," she said.

"Have a goodnight," replied Aunt Sarah.

* * *

Audrey reached home to a warm bed, waiting for her. She lay down peacefully and was about to turn off the light of her small reading lamp when she realised the Book Of Doors was right next to her — on her bedside stool. It was opened to where she had stopped reading. She hadn't realised that she'd come with the book. She could have sworn she'd left it at the Reid House. Audrey picked the rather large book for her little frame. She placed it on her bed and fell asleep while admiring the leather back-cover and the beautiful adornments and markings of the book. She suddenly saw the writing on the page appear. She continued reading from where she had left off.

However, in the morning she realised that it was only a dream and the pages were still missing or blank. She couldn't trust what she read from the dream. She couldn't wait to head over to the Reid House to tell them what had happened. As she was getting ready, she heard a scream from her mother downstairs. "Oh my God, ahhhh!" shouted Audrey's mother again.

"Are you OK, Mummy?" Audrey's jaw dropped. She had never seen her mother lose her cool like that. Audrey's parents were firm believers in the rational and so Audrey was careful never to mention anything supernatural to her mother, but that day it was her mother that would mention something not quite natural. She rushed downstairs as fast as she could and saw her mother, exasperated and out of breath. "I just saw a ghost, my dear," her mother said. She turned on the TV and there was news about people around the world seeing things and panicking. "Do you need me to call Daddy?"

"No, I'll be okay. Luckily it's a Saturday so I don't have to go to work. I think I'm just exhausted," replied Audrey's mother, but she was still watching the news and apparently she wasn't the only one that had seen things. "If everyone keeps seeing things, I think they'll have to close school," she continued, pursed her lips and knitted her eyebrows as she flipped through all the news channels. Audrey couldn't help but smile. Secretly, she would be happy if school closed, so she'd have more time to study the Book of Doors. "Okay Mummy, I'm going to Billy and Segun's house," said Audrey. She hurriedly left the house. Her mother was glad her daughter had made new friends and was no longer all by herself after school in lonely Stony Oak.

* * *

"Sorry guy's I took the book home," said Audrey. She had just arrived at the Reid House.

"No, you didn't. It's right where you left it on the table," replied Segun with his arms akimbo. "Huh?" Audrey shrieked in a high pitched voice she did not recognise. "But I had it with me just a moment ago." She picked up her backpack from the little

basket on her mobility scooter, unzipped it, but it was empty — no Book of Doors.

"The Book of Doors has the ability to appear to whoever it wishes," said a disembodied voice. "Is that Billy's mother?" asked Audrey.

"Yes, it's me Carla," she replied and then materialised.

"You can't move things, can you?" asked Segun.

"That would explain how the book followed me home last night."

"Clever. I'm impressed," responded Carla Reid. She had slipped back into the human world after Segun attempted to do what Billy did with the planchette a few days ago.

"Anyway, time is going. Have you seen the news—ghost everywhere? Can you help?" asked Audrey.

"Of course, that's why I'm here. Where's Billy?"

"Upstairs," answered Segun.

The trio studying the Book of Doors on a rooftop

Six

Kingdom of Azrea

"The day has come when the chosen one must come forward," said Viktor Ripmav, a very skinny man with a curved nose like the beak of a raven. He wore a long black coat that made him even more like a raven. His long black hair didn't help either. It added to the contrast between his dark clothes and his very pale greenish skin. Victor Ripmav looked very scary, but it turned out he was afraid of the dark himself, so the teenagers were not afraid of him.

"I totally agree with you," replied Arthur Broadbottom. He appeared in his usual comical way. This time he tiptoed out of the darkness of one of the open doors and made a 'whoooo' sound as if to frighten in a joky-playful way. The teenagers were no longer afraid of seeing the ghosts as they'd already seen them so many times, but there was one that they'd never seen before. He was the ghost of the fourth door.

"Allow me to introduce myself. I am Rabeus Farabus. I believe this is our first meeting," he said. He had clever eyes, a gentle smile, and a huge belly. He made no elaborate entry. He simply opened the door and walked out.

"No, I've seen you before, but in a dream," said Audrey.

"Is that so?" responded Rabeus Farabus, his clever eyes slightly disappointed. He clasped his fingers and floated over the Book of Doors, which was spread open, and placed on the centre of the table in the Hidden Room. The missing chapter then appeared and Audrey realised the whole chapter was exactly what she dreamt of. The chapter was titled, 'The Trackers' and the first paragraph was all about how the Trackers came together. Audrey's eyes paced through the text from right to left, up to bottom and vice versa. She stopped reading and looked up at the ghosts and then at Billy and Segun. "It says, *'Billy the chosen one, and Audrey and Segun who are by his side, shall one day become apprentices of the Trackers...'* How does it say our names?"

"The book knows many things, Audrey," replied Carla Reid.

"So we are Trackers apprentices?" asked Billy.

"Something like that," responded Arthur Broadbottom.

"So tell us about the worlds," asked Billy, but the ghosts couldn't stay longer. They went back into their respective photographs.

* * *

Days later, the teenagers kept carrying out one test after another and it seemed like there was no end to the trials.

"So what exactly will I do when I get there?" exasperated Billy as he sighed and sat down with a glass of milk. He was more confused than ever. They'd been training for quite a few days and doing so many quizzes with the ghosts, and everyday Audrey performed better than Billy and Segun.

"I don't know, but it's fun, right?" replied Segun.

"When are we going to get into the one of the worlds, I just can't wait," said Billy.

"I think we only have four trials left," said Audrey.

"Only?"

"Yes, according to the book."

"Great! Let's head back to the Hidden Room."

While upstairs, Billy picked up the planchette as he always did, attached the hand of the ballerina into its slot and the room vibrated. The ghosts appeared and the first door opened. Audrey was the first to go through the door, followed by Segun and finally Billy. He was about to turn and close the door when Alfred rushed in. Carla Reid smiled. She was happy the teenagers had finally made it. "Seems like there isn't any lesson left," said Segun. Audrey nodded at him in agreement. "You are most welcome to Azrea but I can't exist here, so your guide will have to be Arthur Broadbottom," said Carla Reid before vanishing.

"Mr Arthur Broadbottom, what are we supposed to do here?" asked Billy, who realised that Arthur Broadbottom was solid and not a ghost anymore.

"In Azrea, there is evil. The elites of the human world have brokered deals with some from here to provide them with power and wealth, and that has caused a problem on this side. We must fix it," replied Arthur Broadbottom.

"So what's Azrea all about anyway?" asked Billy.

"It's a world of witches, wizards, dragons, goblins, orcs, and leprechauns. So many races," replied Arthur Broadbottom.

"Awesome," said Segun. Billy turned around and noticed Segun had grown bigger. "What happened to Segun?"

"Segun has made himself comfortable with this world, that's why. Here, your thoughts instantly affect the way you appear. Remember your cloak spells," replied Arthur Broadbottom.

"Look guys, I can walk properly!" bubbled Audrey while excitedly jumping around. Billy still looked pretty much the same, but he tried the cloak spell and was able to disappear momentarily.

"Alright lads and lass, just convince the king to stop his subjects from making deals with people from our world. Then return to Earth. Remember, only Billy can stay here for a long time. The two of you must return before Sun down."

"Oh yeah, like pausing a video game and taking a piss break?" said Segun.

"I have to go. I can't stay here much longer," responded Arthur Broadbottom with a puzzled look on his face. He probably had no idea what a video game was, thought Segun. Author Broadbottom began oscillating and then disappeared.

"Cute," commented Audrey.

"Remember, Audrey and Segun, you must leave before Sun down. Only Billy can remain here indfinaaa—" shouted Arthur Broadbottom. He had already disappeared, but his voice could still be heard like a trail. It was a warning he left for the teenagers, but unfortunately, they had hardly heard what he said.

"Was that Broadbottom?" asked Billy.

"Sounded like him. I think he was just being silly," replied Audrey.

"Okay, it's not that hard. Let's just go to the castle where the king lives. Tell him what Broadbottom said, and we are done," said Billy.

"Cool, sounds good," replied Audrey.

Azrea was a world of rolling green hills, castles, beautiful floating ships, witches on broomsticks, little goblins, friendly orcs, and talking trees.

"This world looks like low poly but high poly. If that makes sense," observed Segun.

"I see what you mean. It's pretty much how I've always imagined a fantasy world," responded Billy. He looked toward Audrey to hear what she thought about the Kingdom of Azrea but she was lost in excitement about running and walking, and then he had an idea — what if he could fly? He thought about it and there he was up in the air waving at Segun and Audrey, who were still on the ground, but not for long. They also joined Billy and flew across the sky. "Try flying too, Alfred!" screamed Segun. Alfred tried and tried and finally began flying, too. All four of them flew across the picturesque landscapes of Azrea and finally spotted an elaborately decorated masterpiece of a castle. They thought it must be the king's castle, so they got down to the ground and trekked toward it.

"Welcome to Campton Hold. Our king lives here ehi eeee-heee," said a little man with a bulbous pink nose.

"I swear if someone told me I'd be in Super Mario world last week I wouldn't have believed it," said Segun.

"It's actually more like Shrek," replied Audrey.

"Guys, please let's try to blend in," commented Billy. The King's castle was as big as a small town but constructed with a single rock or stone — moulded into place. There were so many creatures and races all going about their businesses peacefully, even elves. Unfortunately, beyond the second gate, they couldn't see anything or anyone anymore. Audrey turned around and noticed all the people had vanished. Alfred ran and climbed the portcullis gear to get a better view of where everyone went, but immediately jumped off after it rotated. They were closing all the gates and putting up the castle's defences.

"What happened to all the people?" asked Segun. All the happy people ran away and the king's knights came out and took their positions.

"Hurry, over here, hiiiide!" cried out a denizen of the castle. He was a strange-looking man with rather large eyes for his small face. "What are we hiding from?" asked Billy.

"We need to hide from the forces of disorder," yelled someone else from a distance. He was hiding under a wooden drum. "I think we should hide," said Segun. They ran and hid together with the man with the strange face. "Does everybody always hide?" asked Audrey.

"Yes everyday around noon, we have to hide when the Dark One passes."

"Who or what is the Dark One?" asked Audrey.

"The Dark One is unknowable, oooh just so scary," replied the man, who was helping them hide. He then transformed from a 'normal looking-strange looking man' into the most hideous creature with an abhorrent smell, a crooked face and an evil laugh. "What is happening to you?" shouted Audrey.

"Remember all the lessons we learnt. They can't harm us, right?" said Segun, not sure if it was a statement or a question and not sure if he believed that. The denizens of Azrea moaned and screamed and rolled on the ground as they transformed. Within a few minutes, all the denizens transformed into the most hideous creatures they'd ever seen. The goblins became massive orcs who plundered and set fire to buildings. leprechauns transformed into hellish insects, and elves transformed into birds of prey with human faces. The beautiful Azrea itself transformed into a land of volcanoes and fire breathing leviathans.

"I think we should go over there. Come on," shouted Alfred. They followed him as he galloped through the ensuing pandemonium. They reached a circular-crystal building where there was relative peace. The only building that seemed impervious to the destruction.

"How did you know to come here Alfred," asked Audrey.

"Just a guess, but hey look. There's no one here," he replied.

"What is this place, anyway?" asked Segun.

"It's called the Looking Glass. It's written outside," replied Billy.

"There is something in the middle of the building. Like a mirror?" asked Audrey.

"Not sure it's a mirror. More like a smooth crystal. Hey look, it has photos. It's my Mum—Carla," Billy looked at a large display at the centre of the white coloured marbled interior. The mirror like crystal showed various images of Carla Reid and finally an image of her heavily pregnant, holding shopping bags. His eyes dilated, and he broke a sweat from the concentration. "That must be when she was about to have you I guess," exclaimed

Audrey. The Looking Glass then blackened and showed a new image. It was Mr Ade's face. He was in a toilet brushing teeth and looking at himself in the mirror. Audrey noticed that when he blinks, the Looking Glass blackens. Mr Ade moved away from the mirror, and only his hands were visible. "I think the Looking Glass can show people's points of view — like how they see the world," she said.

"Looking Glass, show me what my mother is seeing," instructed Audrey. The Looking Glass then showed Audrey's mother busy calling Audrey. Audrey checked her phone but immediately saw the 'no-service' sign. Her mother looked worried and had given Audrey over six missed calls. "Show me Arthur Broadbottom now," commanded Billy, and the large mirror blackened. It was no longer reflective. It then displayed Arthur Broadbottom in the nineteenth century, seated on a barber's chair ready to have a trim. "No, show me Broadbottom now. Where is he?" but the Looking Glass had nothing to show. "Huh?" Segun sighed, he looked confused and then asked, "Show me Pete! As he is now, not before."

"Who is Pete?" asked Audrey.

"His late brother," replied Billy. Segun's command fell on deaf ears. The Looking Glass was black. "This is weird," said Billy. "Come on, let's get out of here."

* * *

Moments later, they emerged from the crystalline womb of the colossal circular building. By then, the commotion had almost stopped and some denizens of Azrea had already trans-formed back to the lovely, cute creatures that they were when the teenagers arrived. "I told you to hide," said the strange-looking man they'd encountered earlier who had given them shelter. He had almost transformed back but still had some scales.

"I am sorry you had to see that," said a man with a long beard and a crown on his head. That must be the king, thought Billy. "Are you the King?" he asked.

"Yes, I am. Whenever the Dark One passes, this happens."

"I could not see the Dark One," responded Billy.

"It was just sundown," blurted Audrey.

"Shh! Don't give them reasons to suspect us," Alfred sibilated.

"Sun? And what might that be? You must be outsiders from Takrea" said the king with a suspicious expression on his face.

"Tak—what? More like 'Earth-rea'," jested Segun.

"Normally, I would have ordered you to be thrown in to the dungeons but now even the heathens from Takrea are running here. The Dark One is a scourge. No one seems to get away from," the king said, his eyes teary as he looked at the destructions caused by the Dark One.

"We came to tell you to stop your subjects from making deals with humans from Earth. Otherwise, the Dark One will keep on coming—I guess. Please tell them to stop." Billy cleverly explained to the King, but the King hardly understood what Billy was talking about. "I don't quite understand what you are saying, outsider, but if it will help stop the Dark One, then I'll listen to you," replied the King. "Put to death all who speak with outsiders. Particularly visitors from invisible worlds," said the King. He passed a Royal Edict and newspapers were printed as well as posters pasted on every door throughout the Kingdom of

Azrea.The purpose of the posters was to warn the people of the kingdom against making deals with people from Earth.

The teenagers thought they did well. They made their way back to the entry point where the door that would take them back to the Hidden Room should be. It was in a cookie shop, exactly where they arrived at, but on the way Audrey noticed that the sun hadn't moved since they arrived. She remembered Billy had observed that the Dark One was actually just night-time. Clearly, night time differed completely from the way it was on earth, she thought. She also recalled Arthur Broadbottom's warning. "Hurry, I think we stayed longer than a day!" she shouted.

"No way, we've only been here for like an hour," replied Segun.

"Lets fly," shouted Billy.

They flew back to the cookie shop and opened the door. Audrey's left leg became ghostly, while Segun couldn't feel his arm. Billy glanced at Alfred and noticed he was turning green.

When they returned to the Hidden Room, Audrey had nose bleeds while Segun had a terrible headache. Alfred was just an ordinary dog again, but Billy was fine, just as Arthur Broadbottom cautioned.

Arthur Broadbottom sitting in the Hidden Room

Seven

Regroup

Days passed without Audrey visiting the Reid House. Though she'd see Billy in class and Segun on break-time now and then but they never spoke about their trip to the Kingdom of Azrea or even about the Hidden Room anymore. Like Audrey always said, 'what's the point'. She knew nobody would believe it, anyway. Segun attempted to write an essay about their trip in his English class but only got a pass mark for it. "Nice try, Segun, but not convincing," said one boy in his class.

"Yeah, out here talking 'bout goblins and shit haha," said another boy, and the whole class erupted in laughter. "At least my essay is just fiction, but your parents are actually seeing ghosts, haha," Segun retorted, defending himself, which also made the class erupt in laughter. "Alright, settle down, class. It's all just mass hysteria. I'm glad Segun is being creative with it, though," said Miss Amanda. She was the only teacher Segun really liked, even though English wasn't really one of his strong points. Too bad he couldn't impress her, he thought.

"Thanks miss Amanda," said Segun.

"It's fine. Just work on your spellings," she said. Soon after, Segun went on break and saw Audrey in the cafeteria. He picked up a tray, got a plate of mashed potatoes, sausages, and gravy with a cup of orange juice, and headed over to share a table with her.

"Talk about being saved by the bell," complained Segun with a sigh of relief.

"Oh, tell me about it. My class is so boring," Audrey concurred.

"How are you anyway?" asked Segun, while touching his phone and scrolling through Audrey's Instagram page. "Can't see any uploads from you lately," he added.

"You mean since Kingdom of Azrea?"

"Yeah, I mean like in general, yeah," replied Segun, still avoiding Audrey's eyes.

"Are you trying to invite me to the Hidden Room?" asked Audrey, slightly excited.

At that moment, Billy emerged from a passing crowd. "We agreed you guys can't travel anymore. I took the book back," said Billy.

"But we don't need the book to travel," replied Segun.

"Listen, it's not safe, Segun."

"He's right, Segun," bewailed Audrey, her face expressionless, trying to hide her sadness.

"Wait a minute, what's happening?" screamed Segun, making a few people turn their heads to look at their table.

"What's going on?" both Billy and Audrey asked in unison.

"It's my exercise book. There's a map that just appeared!"

"A map of what? It was probably there all along," replied Billy, looking around to see if Segun had raised more alarms. "It says Map of the Kingdom of Azrea."

"Hmm, strange. You guys are still not travelling, ever again," responded Billy. Segun glanced at Audrey. They both knew that the map wasn't there before.

* * *

Billy, prepared for his trip. He was more convinced than ever of his role in everything, and he knew exactly what to do. As soon as he got home, he turned on the TV and there was still news now and then of someone from some part of the world who saw a ghost. Things were getting out of hand, he thought.

"Just absolute madness, eh, Billy," said Arthur Broadbottom.

"Yeah, Audrey's mum saw a ghost too," replied Billy.

"That's why we must hurry," commented Carla Reid, who had just appeared from behind the second door. "Mum, I'm travelling alone today. It's too dangerous for Audrey and Segun."

"I understand, my love. That is why I brought you this ring. If you point it at Segun and Audrey, it can send them right back to the point of entry," said Carla Reid as she gently placed the magical ring on the table in the centre of the Hidden Room.

"So they can leave without staying for too long," replied Billy with a look of hope on his face. He picked up the ring and examined it closely. The ring had a large gemstone and on the undergallery or underneath the gemstone, Billy saw an etched word. "Raco?" he asked, reading the etched word.

"That is correct. This is the family tradition. I'm so proud of you, Billy." said Carla Reid.

"The next world you must travel to is called Caput Amore," said Arthur Broadbottom. He placed his ghostly foot on the chair, leaned forward with his hand on his chin and his eyeballs moving from right to left. "This one is difficult, O' boy," he continued.

"More monsters?" asked Billy.

"No, not at all," replied Arthur Broadbottom.

"Just love. Too much of it. It's the place where lovers' hearts yearn for," said Carla Reid. Her cheeks flushed red, her eyes darted around, and she extended her ghostly hand and gently embraced Billy's face. Then she performed a jeté and an entrechat — basically all the movements of a ballerina, which made Billy recall the porcelain and how he shattered it into a million pieces. Carla Reid grabbed a ghostly rose and kissed it and placed it in an empty dusty jar. The rose lasted for about a minute and then disappeared. "Oh, just thinking about Caput Amore is so captivating," she added.

"Caput Amore is also where the spirits of lovers travel to at night," said Arthur Broadbottom. "I just hope Billy can return in one piece."

"So there are no monsters and it's full of love. Is that all?," asked Billy.

"There is an evil queen," replied Carla Reid.

"When souls travel there at night, they can't return," said Arthur Broadbottom.

"Souls from Earth?" asked Billy.

"Yes, yes. The queen is stealing lovers' hearts in their sleep.

Literaaaally." replied Carla Reid. She hummed, sat in a corner
and then floated all over the room while singing.

"It began on a lonely Autumn Morning:
I was the most Knowing Tracker around.
She was the most Alluring Queen.

She was my enemy.
My alluring enemy,
My queen.

We used to run so well together,
Back then.
We wanted to smile together around the world,
We wanted it all.

But one morning, one lonely morning.
We smiled too much.
Together we listened to a frog.
It was fast, so fast.

From that moment, our relationship changed.
She grew so distant.

And then it happened:

Oh, no! Oh, no!

She kissed a lover.

Alas, a lover!
My enemy kissed a lover.
It was loving, so loving.

The next day I thought my heart had broken,
I thought my ears had burst into flames,
(But I was actually overreacting a little.)

Even so, she is in my thoughts.
I think about how it all changed that morning,
That lonely autumn morning.

My ears… ouch!
When I think of that alluring queen,
That alluring queen and me."

* * *

"Oh, that was something," said Billy, "so I'm supposed to stop the queen. How?"

"Just break the chains that cage the central library," replied Arthur Broadbottom.

"The library was built thousands of years ago. It is the only way to enlighten the people," commented Carla Reid. "There are more emotions and feelings to experience other than just love and take this sword," she added.

"If we don't stop that, all lovers will disappear from Earth and end up there," cautioned Arthur Broadbottom. Billy nodded. He then placed the hand of the ballerina in its slot in the planchette, and then the room vibrated and the second door opened. He stepped in to Caput Amore. Wow, it's beautiful, he thought. His eyes fell in love with the stars, the trees, the grass, and even the tiniest ants. Everything was so beautiful in Caput Amore. The colours were vivid, and many did not exist on Earth.

* * *

Meanwhile, Audrey had just returned home from school. She dropped her bag on the carpeted floor of her room and was getting ready to step into the shower when she heard barking outside. She was already half dressed, so she couldn't go downstairs straight away. Instead, she peeped through her window and saw Alfred barking and looking right up at her. "Alfred, are you okay? Is everything OK?" she yelled down from her window overlooking the garden. From a distance stood the Reid family home looking uneventful from the outside. What could be going on? She thought. She got dressed and hurriedly went downstairs to see Alfred, who began to run toward the Reid House. While Audrey sped off on her mobility scooter after Alfred. She nearly bumped into an old woman who was crossing the road. "Are you travelling through the Hidden Room, my dear?" The old woman asked. She was wearing a black velvet coat. "What? How do you know?" asked Audrey.

"Oh, I was there last week helping Segun's mum with some tasks. I saw you go in and vanished," she replied.

"Errm, errm," Audrey was lost for words.

"I know they told you, you can't stay longer in Azrea but that's not true. You can get used to it, you know," the old lady responded and vanished into the nearby shrubs across the road.

Audrey carried on without looking back to see where the old lady went. She reached the Reid House shortly after and saw Segun and Alfred waiting for her outside. "He left without us. Let's go," said Segun. That must be why Alfred came to get her, she thought.

* * *

Meanwhile, Billy had reached the central library at Caput Amore, a massive building with lovely architecture — just as lovely as everything else, but he knew it wasn't time for admiring the city. Billy recalled the warnings about not looking at anyone or risk falling in love with them. Standing by an enormous golden door of the central library, he raised the sword he was given by Arthur Broadbottom; but just as he raised it, he noticed the lock itself and the chains were so beautiful. He decided it would be too cruel to strike such a wonderful chain. Instead, he used a window and accessed the Central Library. He had hoped he'd be able to find relevant books the evil queen had hidden from her people. Where is Audrey when you need her? There must be like a million books in here. She could have easily found the relevant ones, he thought. So, he decided to go back and get Audrey and Segun since now he had a magical ring, which could send them back anytime. He hurriedly returned to the point of entry into Caput Amore, which was a beautiful bathhouse with steam and bubbles everywhere. He lowered his head and walked through in order not to see anyone, but his eyes trailed and he saw the most beautiful little cat he'd ever seen. Billy decided to look at the cat for just a few seconds since he was so close to the door, but the cat's owner picked it up. It was a girl around

Billy's age. "I see you admire my cat," she said. She was dressed in pearls and a white lace, her turquoise eyes sparkling like the sea at sunset. "Come princess, time to go," the maid of the princess called out. He turned around and saw hundreds of her admirers posted up like zombies, but luckily he could snap out of it in time to leave Caput Amore.

* * *

Billy returned to the Hidden Room and met Audrey and Segun waiting for him. "What's the big idea leaving without us?" Segun asked a rhetorical question.

"Well, I just... I mean... It was for your own good," responded Billy.

"What's that smirk on your face?" asked Audrey. Billy dropped his new sword on the table and his new ring.

"I was at Caput Amore. It's behind door number two," he replied. Both Audrey and Segun could hardly imagine what that world was like since they'd never been. Segun rubbed his palm on the wall where door number two was. The positions of three doors were on one wall, while a lone door was by itself on a different wall. The Hidden Room was indeed a mysterious place, thought Segun. Although he was more curious about Billy's facial expression.

"They make you smile over there?" asked Segun, but Billy ignored that question.

"Listen guys, I need your help," said Billy.

"Look, Segun's map is real. The one that appeared in his notebook. It wasn't there before," said Audrey, "and an old lady I met on the way here said it's possible to stay longer in the worlds."

"I know and you can come with me, anyway. This ring can send you back anytime, so it's OK," replied Billy as he attempted to put the ring on his ring finger, but it was too big. He tried his middle finger, but it was still too big. He even tried to put the ring on his thumb, but it just wouldn't stay, so he attached it to his bracelet.

"So, like it or not, we are coming with you next time. Maybe we will smile like that too when we come back," said Segun, still pressing on and grinning.

Eight

Volkodlakea

The road so far

"This castle is your point of entry. I'll do my best to protect you here in this accursed place," said Viktor Ripmav, his contorted face partially lit by the light of the moon and the other half in darkness, his frail hands always cracking by the joints, and his bent spine barely able to support the weight of his head. He wore a dark robe and recommended that they wear something similar. "Remember, your spells do not work here," he cautioned.

"Yes, I remember that from the lessons," commented Audrey. Viktor Ripmav acknowledged.

"This used to be the world I come from, my home, but I joined the Trackers when I learnt the truth. No longer was I to remain so carnal," said Viktor Ripmav as he ran his long non-human nails into the cracks of the walls of the castle. Lightning and thunder followed, which illuminated the darkened room and revealed a framed photo of Viktor Ripmav on the wall. "This was your castle," commented Billy.

"You are a vampire?" asked Audrey, a bit scared.

"Don't be afraid. I mean you no harm," responded Viktor Ripmav. At which point Segun thought Alfred made the right choice by giving this trip a pass.

"So, what do we do here?" asked Billy.

"In this world, unfortunately, humans are cattle for vampires. It wasn't like that before," replied Viktor Ripmav.

"Cattle..." commented Audrey.

"Yes, ever since the last elf went extinct, that was all," responded Viktor Ripmav.

Volkodlakea was a horrible place, humans laboured on the streets and farmed other humans for vampires to make use of. It was a nightmare. The streets were littered with human bones, but Volkodlakia did not start out that way. Thousands of years ago, it was a world of indescribable beauty, populated by humans and elves. Unfortunately, so many racial wars between elves and humans were fought— with humans always at the receiving end. However, one day, a human scientist worked hard enough to produce a weapon that would kill all elves. It worked, but unfortunately, it transformed him into the first vampire. The human scientist now a vampire, then went on to infect so many humans with vampirism. Many of the elves were wiped out, and then the vampires turned on humans.

"So back in the Hidden Room, Arthur Broadbottom said the vampires can't harm us. Is that correct?" asked Billy.

"Yes, we have to go down to the dungeons of this castle. I have kept some elves in there—secretly," replied Viktor Ripmav.

"I thought the elves were all extinct," commented Audrey.

"Not all," replied Viktor Ripmav.

"So we could have been killed coming here?" asked Segun as they boarded an old lift that used a system of pulleys weighed down by buckets of water. They arrived at the lowest sub-ground floor where the dungeons were, and finally located the lab where the elves were kept in suspended animation.

"Don't worry, you are fine. I will give you a concoction of vampire blood, elf blood as well as this serum. If you drink it, the vampires will not be able to tell you are humans," said Viktor Ripmav. He drew blood out from a sleeping elf child and then drew out his own blood. He added the two into a mixture and placed it in a test tube.

"So are there any elf-vamps?" asked Segun.

"No, the elven blood does not agglutinate. It runs like water even after death," replied Viktor Ripmav.

"So, it can never mix with vampire blood," concluded Audrey.

"Exactly. It's like water and oil. Therefore, when I add this magical serum to it, it can take out the vampire curse. Leaving only the human blood and the elf blood," Viktor Ripmav exulted, raising the serum in the air to catch the light of burning torches.

"This is the cure," said Billy.

"Yes, that is why I need you to go find Volkrod Wilkenhold — the castle of the first vampire."

The teenagers made their way back up to the ground floor. Viktor Ripmav was about to leave when Segun called out to him, "Wait," he said, "why can't we just leave them alone? They ain't done nothing wrong!"

"Some from Earth, have made deals with sorcerers to live two lifetimes. This type of sorcery involves the blood of the vampires. In exchange, the vampires receive human blood from Earth, which makes them even more powerful," explained Viktor Ripmav but Segun just turned his head from right to left, he still couldn't see the logic in that. "It's their world and we have ours. Who cares?" he protested.

"The humans here are innocent Segun, come on let's go," responded Billy.

* * *

They moved through the streets of Volkodlakea, and the vampires did not notice them. Enough time had passed that the sun should have risen, but it didn't. There was a large monument at the centre of the city called the monument of the moon. It was commemorating the first vampire who defeated the elves, and blackened the sky to a perpetual night. Blood was cascading down from the monument.

"What is this?" Billy asked a passerby.

"This is a fountain, dummy. Drink, it's free, boy," replied the passerby, a mean-looking character with a hairy chest. "They must have a lot of human blood," said Segun.

"I think they manufacture it. Broadbottom said they farmed humans here," responded Audrey.

"Yup," said Segun.

"I think we can find a way to Volkrod Wilkenhold from here," said Billy, pointing at a narrow path that went up toward a castle. On the way up, vampires whispered and giggled as they consumed human blood. For them, it was a perfect world, no different from humans' farming and eating chickens. The sky was still dark even though it should have been daytime. How did they do it? Billy wondered, and then raised his head and looked up. He noticed a black smoke was floating up in the atmosphere — blackening the sky. Audrey had noticed it too. "I think they are burning something. Could it be fossil fuels?" she assumed.

"No way, it would have run out," said Segun. The teenagers walked up a narrow path toward the castle and finally arrived at an entrance where many humans were being shipped in and vampires were gathering to go into an auditorium. "Are you here for the show?" asked a little vampire boy. "No — I mean, yes we are," Segun answered quickly.

"What show is it?" Billy asked.

"Are you not from around here?" asked the little vampire.

"We are," replied Audrey.

"It's a human circus," responded the little vampire. "Humans are so good at performing tricks," he added. Little did he know that Billy, Audrey and Segun were human and were, in fact, tricking them at that very moment. They eluded the entire vampire security and reached the highest row in the auditorium where they could see the stage. "I think the vampire king sits over there," said Billy. "if I use this projectile to inject the vampire king with the serum, it will cure all vampires."

"Be careful," replied Audrey.

"Wait a minute, you believe that weirdo, Ripmav? What if it doesn't work?" asked Segun in a hushed voice. Billy leaned nearer to Segun and whispered, "I have the ring that my mother gave me, remember? We can return to Ripmav's castle at anytime." The vampire king arrived and was led to the stage where he addressed the crowd. "I am Bracanzee the lord of vampires. It is I who brought victory against the evil elves. It is I who wiped them out. It I who made us strong, fast, and healthy. It is I who made us SUPERIOR!" yelled the vampire king Brancanzee. His large fangs catching the light of burning torches. He raised his arms up as the crowd cheered and the circus began.

Before he reached his designated seat, he stopped, his nose twitching and his brow even more wrinkled than before. "I smell humans in the crowd. All humans must only be on stage! Find them," he thundered. The vampires began to look around and a special team of 'spotters' were sent to find the humans in the auditorium. Billy was about to use his ring, but as he readied himself, he noticed Segun had followed someone.

"This way, follow me. I can help you," whispered a hooded figure. Billy nodded, turned around, and motioned for Audrey to follow him. They both followed Segun, who was following the hooded person. The four of them dispersed into the crowds and made an exit under a seat. "Who are you?" asked Billy as he followed closely behind the hooded figure.

"I'll explain everything later," responded the hooded figure. They passed through tunnels and tunnels of twisted corridors until they arrived at a river at the base of the castle. The hooded figure removed their hoodie. "It's you," said Audrey.

"You know her?" asked Segun.

"I saw her on Earth,"

"Who are you?" asked Billy.

"I am Raco," she replied. Her silverly-brown hair flowing in the wind. Audrey noticed that she was now much younger than she was when she bumped into her on the way to the Reid House. "Well Raco, thanks for getting us out of there," commented Billy, "speaking of which, I think this is a good time to use the ring and get Audrey and Segun back home," he added.

"You don't have to go just yet. There is a way you can recharge and stay longer," said Raco, "whatever world you visit, just find the central stone."

"The central stone?" asked Audrey.

"Yes, even Earth has a central stone," she replied.

"So, some people on Earth are really from a different dimension," concluded Segun.

"That is correct," she responded.

"So that can buy us more time to defeat Bracanzee," said Billy.

"I must go now. See you again and godspeed," she said and jumped into a wormhole.

"Whoah, how cool is that?" exclaimed Segun.

* * *

They returned to Viktor Ripmav's castle and went straight to his sub-ground laboratory to confront him about his 'not so effective serum'. They searched everywhere, but Viktor Ripmav was nowhere to be found. Finally, Segun said he thought it would be a good idea to go back home but as they made their way out of the lab, they discovered it was surrounded by vampires. "There they are, seize them," shouted Brancanzee. They ran back into the castle and ran upstairs to Viktor Ripmav's room and opened his closet door where they had entered Volkodlakea from, but it didn't work. They were still in the closet and the vampires were approaching fast.

"Over there. They are hiding there," yelled one vampire who could smell them as the effect of the serum wore off even more. "Great, chain them and take them back to my castle. Mwhahaha hahah hahaha," Brancanzee crackled loudly.

Over at the castle, they were thrown in cages and questioned. "I am not going to ask again. I know you are part of the resistance. Tell me where the other humans are. Tell me," Brancanzee's deputy screamed.

"We don't know what you are talking about, honestly," responded Billy.

"Haha, you think you can lie to me, human?" screamed Brancanzee's right-hand man again. "Enough!" shouted Brancanzee. "Hold my robe," he said, handing over his robe to an assistant. He revealed his fur covered torso. "I don't want to get any blood on my robe when I consume these succulent humans, mwhahahah." The cage was opened and Billy was thrown out. Brancanzee grabbed Billy's neck and raised him up, showing him to the whole crowd, then he sunk his massive fangs into Billy's neck. The whole crowd cheered in glorious ovation. Unfortunately for Brancanzee, the serum was still in Billy's blood. He coughed and wriggled on the floor in anguish. "What is happening to me, I feel... I feel so... weak... I feel so human..." Brancanzee transformed into a human and the whole crowd of thousands of vampires was dead silent.

"Billy, are you okay?" screamed Audrey as she burst out of the cage.

"Yes, I'm ok. His saliva healed my wound," replied Billy, rubbing his neck.

"No, I mean, are you human?"

"I still feel human, alright," replied Billy.

"Come on. Let's get out of here," quavered Segun. He was visibly terrified, but the vampires were getting nearer and nearer—closing in on the dungeon's entrance. "Wait a minute, I know a secret path," said Brancanzee who was now in his normal, 'feeble' human body like he had been before transforming into the first vampire.

They used the secret path to arrive safely at Viktor Ripmav's castle and this time, the door to the Hidden Room was accessible. Brancanzee formed an alliance with some of the elves that were kept at Viktor Ripmav's castle. Together they formed a coalition of elves and humans to recover Volkodlakea from the vampires and return it to its former glory. The resistance was named Humans and Elves for Volkadlakea (HEV).

Nine

The Lost Souls

It was a bright sunny day but oddly enough; it started out with light showers. Billy looked up at the clock mounted on the wall above his classroom's whiteboard. It was nearly two o'clock and his heart sunk. He couldn't wait to go back home so he could go to the Hidden Room and travel somewhere so he could help his mother move on to her next life. As much as he was enjoying seeing her, he knew she'd have to leave, eventually. There was also the case of teachers seeing ghosts around the school. Last week his science teacher screamed after seeing a ghost while alone marking students' homework after school.

"Is your mother still seeing ghosts Audrey?" Billy asked Audrey as they got on the school bus to head home after school. "Yeah, I think the house is haunted," replied Audrey. Billy looked worried. He felt responsible somehow, and he knew he had to take the matter more urgently. He knew they needed to do all what the Trackers were telling them to do. "I think we should read The Book of Doors again," said Billy.

"Why is that?" asked Segun, who had his headphones on but had apparently been listening to them from the back of the bus. The bus was now empty because they were the last kids to be dropped off as they lived the farthest. "Well, I think we could find some shortcuts, or answers." responded Billy.

"Why can't we just listen to the Trackers?" blurted Audrey, "and whatever happened to Volkodlakea?" Billy turned around and looked at Segun as if to say, what is she talking about? "Volkodlakea? Maybe all vampires are human again with the help of Brancanzee," he replied with a look of content on his face.

"I don't think so," replied Segun.

"Why not?" asked Billy.

"I think nothing we do really matters. We are just kids," responded Segun.

"I'm not a kid. I'm almost fourteen—" replied Billy.

"And no matter what little we can do. It matters," interjected Audrey.

"So why are people still seeing ghosts? Why is the Dark One still destroying Azrea? I think the only little help we offered was in Volkodlakea,"

"Yeah, you right. It's all quite confusing," Billy replied, as the bus reached a stop by the junction between Audrey's house and the Reid House. "Alright, see you guys later," said Audrey. They got off the bus and headed home.

* * *

Later that day, Audrey arrived at the Reid House finding Mr

Ade telling Billy and Segun about Billy's mother. "Her favorite colour was green, haha. She was just like your friend Audrey, who likes green too," he joked. Audrey blushed at the sound of her name coming from Mr Ade's lips. "Well, good to know more about mum, I guess," replied Billy.

"So why doesn't she ever wear green?" said Segun, perplexed. "She's always wearing white whenever she comes."

"Huh? Do you know who we are talking about? She's long gone," yelped Mr Ade.

"Errm, Segun means, in pictures. We've seen a few of her photographs in the basement," Billy suddenly sputtered, trying to throw Mr Ade off, whose face was deadpanned. Mr Ade, still looking confused, burst out laughing. "Haha, okay, okay. I'm going to take a nap," he said. The three teenagers then made their way to the Hidden Room. Mr Ade heard them going in while getting comfortable in his bed. He smiled comfortably as he took an afternoon siesta.

Billy picked up the planchette as usual and placed the ballerina's hand inside the slot. The room vibrated and the fourth door opened but none of the Trackers were around. There was an eerie green glow coming out of the door. "Is that a world?" asked Audrey.

"No, it's not," replied Billy. "I think it's like a little place before the world."

"That is correct. It is a pocket dimension. This place connects to all worlds," commented Rabeus Frarabus. He appeared on the other side of the fourth door. "A what now?" asked Audrey.

"This is where Billy met his mother when he went missing in London," responded Rabeus Farabus.

"So it all connects," said Billy as he walked through the door. Segun and Audrey followed suit. "Why is it greenish and why are there floating orbs?" asked Audrey..

"In this dimension, there is no bodily pain. Only emotional, psychological and other forms of mental traumas," responded Rabeus Farabus as he ran his hands through his long beard. By then Billy's mother, Carla Reid, appeared wearing a green dress. Segun noticed the green dress and wondered if she was listening to the conversation they had with Mr Ade earlier.

Arthur Broadbottom and Viktor Ripmav also emerged. Behind the green glow, the pocket dimension revealed itself. There were benches and roads as well as buildings. Billy's eyes focused and adjusted to the world and he could see clearer. "The green glow is not so distracting anymore," he observed.

"Yes, I can see too. Look, it's a shop, but what are all these orbs?" asked Audrey.

"The obs are souls of the departed from all four primary worlds," replied Carla Reid. She moved rapidly toward a corner and the greenish clouds that were there dispersed, revealing a set of tables and chairs. It turns out they were inside a cafeteria.

"Huh? This is our school's cafeteria," noticed Segun.

"How is it here?" asked Billy.

"There is a copy of everything from all the worlds in this pocket dimension. It is this dimension that pulls all the worlds close together — it ties everything." replied Carla Reid.

"Great observations from all three of you," exclaimed Rabeus Farabus. "Now look again," he added. As they looked, they noticed the floating orbs had now become people, albeit still with a greenish glowing aura around them. "So, this is now your world? Where all four of you live?" asked Audrey.

"Yes," responded Viktor Ripmav, "that is why you couldn't find me in my castle in Volkodlakea when you were running away from Brancanzee and his minions."

"Is this purgatory?" asked Billy.

"Yes, it is. Sort of, but it isn't supposed to be," replied Rabeus Farabus.

"So all ghosts come here?" asked Billy.

"Yes, my boy," replied Rabeus Farabus.

"If that's so, then why are people still seeing ghosts on Earth? Why isn't this world attracting all the ghosts back here?" asked Segun while he shook his head, habitually.

"Brilliant question! Well, that is why the three of you are here to help." replied Rabeus Farabus.

"We need you to help fix everything," said Carla Reid. She snapped her fingers and the school's cafeteria disappeared and instead they were outside in a park surrounded by children playing in the playground and farther down teenagers fighting. "You both have lost your blood brothers to gang violence," she added.

"That's my brother," shouted Billy.

"And that's Pete, too," screamed Segun, who also spotted his brother.

"Both of them are here in this world. Wouldn't it be nice if they moved somewhere lovely?" said Rabeus Farabus with a smile.

"So they both can't move on," commented Audrey.

"That's right Audrey," said Carla Reid. She snapped her fingers again, and they appeared in an infernal place with sounds of people screaming, shouting and crying. "What is this, Hell?" asked Billy.

"Sure looks like it," bleated Segun. "What are we doing here?" he asked.

"Not to worry, dear Segun. You are not dead. So nothing can harm you here," replied Carla Reid.

"What we need you to do is to make this realm work the way it was supposed to," said Viktor Ripmav who had been quiet all along.

"And what's that?" asked Billy.

"You are children, so you are pure. That's why only you can exist here without being in some sort of hell or another. Your mind creates the hell. You are mostly pure, you haven't sucked a man dry yet. You haven't gorged anyone's eyes yet, you haven't... you haven't—"

"That's enough Ripmav! Carla, I think they've seen enough," Arthur Braodbottom blurted. He had been uneasy since he appeared. He tucked in his shirt properly and wiped sweat off of his forehead and cleared his throat. "Heavens, these fires are Mephistophelian," he added. Carla Reid snapped her fingers, and they appeared in a void space with nothing but a door. Segun was the first to reach the door. He opened it and saw that it led to the Hidden Room. "Ah, what a relief," he said with a sigh.

* * *

Moments later, as the three of them sat in the Hidden Room talking about all they had seen, Audrey had an idea. "What if we brought the lovely little creatures from Azrea to Vokodlakea? I think that would bring peace there," she said.

"I don't think they'll survive there," replied Billy.

"So what exactly is it they want us to do? I still don't get it," asked a confused Segun.

"How many times do they need to explain, Segun? It's about maintaining the balance," replied Audrey.

"Oh yeah, well, what does that mean, smart alec?"

"Look, Segun. They are right. I have the Book of Doors here. It says a balance must be maintained between the worlds," responded Audrey.

"Hmm, I have nothing to say," replied Segun.

"Segun, I know you are scared. You've seen Pete out there, but we have to finish this," Billy reassured Segun. He picked up the planchette and was just about to place the ballerina's hand inside the slot when the third door flung open, followed by a cracking sound. A pinkish cloud poured in and flowers instantly blossomed on top of bookshelves and on the wooden floor. The cracking sounds continued, and the walls of the old house squeaked. The Hidden Room rotated from right to left and even from top to bottom before it came to a stop. The teenagers noticed that the room was illuminated by daylight. The window that had been on the ceiling was now on the wall by the right hand-side. "Are those sounds of gears?" Segun leaned on the wall and placed his left ear on it. "Yes, I think so," replied Audrey.

"Look, I think there's someone coming out," said Billy as he stood in front of the third door. The pink clouds cleared out. A young lady was standing by the door. "Who are you?" asked Audrey. The young girl who had a blueish hue to her skin, pointy ears and clad in body armour stepped into the room. "I am

Princess Mabila and I am from Caput Amore," she said, standing tall and strong.

"I have seen you before," replied Billy. Segun and Audrey glanced at each other as they had never seen Princess Mabila before because they hadn't yet travelled to Caput Amore.

"There is no love in Caput Amore anymore. Every millennium, the Dark One takes love away and the princess or prince must come to Earth to collect love from the spring of love," she said while staring at the walls of the old house.

"Have you been here before?" asked Audrey.

"No, it's my first time," replied the princess.

"Where is the spring?" asked Audrey.

"It should be here in the garden," replied the princess.

"But how do you know if you've never been here before?" asked Segun.

"I was given a map by the librarian," she replied.

"The librarian?" asked Billy.

"Yes, Raco," replied Princess Mabila. She moved away from the door. It closed completely.

"I can show you the garden," said Billy.

"Don't worry, I have the map of the garden and this machine," she replied.

"What machine?" asked Segun as he followed her closely.

"This house, of course," she replied. She moved an old mirror that was mounted on the wall of the Hidden Room and pulled a lever which revealed an entryway with a spiralling set of staircase that led straight to the garden. The lever caused the house to crack and squeak again. This time around, all the noise from the old gears and hinges of the Reid House awoke Mr Ade from his afternoon nap.

"What on earth is that?" he exclaimed as he turned in his sleep. Aunt Sarah had just returned home and was about to rest on her massage chair when she heard the cracking sounds, too. It was Alfred that had welcomed her with his loud barking. He was barking because he had seen the princess from Caput Amore. He knew she came from somewhere beyond the Hidden Room, but he couldn't help barking because he was still a dog. Aunt Sarah went upstairs to alert Mr Ade about all the cracking sounds.

"I know, Sarah, I've heard it too, but we must tolerate it. It's an old house," he said.

"I guess so," Aunt Sarah agreed. On looking out the master bedroom window overlooking the garden, she saw the children. She was glad they'd made another friend who she thought was into cosplay. "Oh, look at their new friend. She's beautiful," commented Aunt Sarah. Mr Ade looked out the window before entering the toilet to take a shower, but the princess had already moved away from his range of vision.

"This is the spring of love," the princess said as she knelt down near the fountain in the garden of the Reid House. "Amazing," said Audrey. The princess brought out leather covered bottles from her bag and filled them with the water flowing from the fountain.

"Wait a minute, the Trackers said, there shouldn't be too much love in Caput Amore or people from Earth go there in their sleep and are unable to return," said Billy. He stood in front of Princess Mabila as if he was trying to stop her from fetching the water from the fountain.

"Out of my way."

Ten

Limuria

"Oh man, that princess was hot," said Segun, while walking down from the supermarket. Billy was stacking the trolley and getting ready to push it to the car park. "Well, you are lucky you haven't visited Caput Amore then," replied Billy. He started manoeuvring the heavy trolley—carefully not to crash into people in the busy Sunday morning. "Oh yeah, why's that?" responded Segun, who was on his phone while walking beside Billy.

"In Caput Amore, you can't look at anyone or risk falling in love with them."

"So they don't have thieves, killers, wicked people?"

"I guess they don't. People spend their times loving others," replied Billy. Aunt Sarah overheard the boys' conversation and commented, "Who wouldn't want to live there?" Billy and Segun bursted out laughing awkwardly and then kept quiet for the rest of the journey back home. While she wondered what active imaginations they must have had.

* * *

Later on, upon returning home, they noticed the grandfather clock had moved away from the wall, revealing the opened door of the Hidden Room. They climbed halfway up the stairs, reaching the landing and peered in to the room, realising that Audrey had already beaten them to it. She was already inside, studying the contents of the Book of Doors carefully. The room was now spotless, and no longer had any dusts or cobwebs since the princess arrived. Mr Ade, who was at home that morning — though getting ready for work—, glanced inside quickly and said, "Well done, guys. You've cleaned that room very well," as he happily ambled down the stairs.

"Alright guys, time to go somewhere," said Billy. He placed the hand of the ballerina inside the planchette, and the room vibrated and the fourth door opened. Carla Reid emerged, followed by Rabeus Farabus, and Arthur Broadbottom, but Viktor Ripmav was missing. Authur Bradbottom was not as jovial as he always was. Instead, he seemed very serious. "It has come to our attention that the Dark One has contacted you," said Arthur Broadbottom. "He has?" gasped Billy, partially curious and partly terrified.

"Indeed, the Dark One operates in a rather topsy-turvy manner. If time and space permit, I would like to tell you about how the Dark One deceived me when I was an adolescent about your age," said Arthur Broadbottom. He fixed his necktie —

characteristically, pulled out a chair and sat down. "We are listening," said Segun.

"He beguiled me by manifesting as a fine young lady who began lally-gagging."

"Lally-what now?" asked Audrey.

"Her behaviour was coquettish," responded Arthur Broadbottom, but he only confused the teenagers even more with his Victorian Era slangs. "Flirting," said Carla Reid, seeing as they clearly weren't following what Arthur Broadbottom was saying. "Oh, okay. We understand," responded the teenagers in unison.

"So, in my folly I was courted by the young lady and I fell for it hook, line, and sinker. My feelings for her grew more and more and she told me about Earth's central stone and that I must help her find so she could save her world. The end was disastrous," sighed Arthur Broadbottom.

"You see, that is why we told you to be careful about outsiders from other worlds," said Carla Reid.

"A princess from Caput Amore was here," exclaimed Audrey.

"Yes, about the princess. Her intentions were likely noble. I doubt it was the machinations of the Dark One—though it could be," said Arthur Broadbottom.

Rabeus Farabus was itching to speak. He looked at Carla Reid as if to say it was his turn. "On a lighter note, today you shall journey to Limuria where I came from," the lighthearted Rabeus Farabus finally uttered the words. He floated across the room and sat near Segun. Putting his ghostly arm around him, he said, "I know you always have questions. So I'll tell you exactly what you need to do there."

"Oh, good to know what's going on, for once," replied Segun

with a stubborn grin on his face. "All you need to do is to go where the Moon sleeps and open the lock that now holds her captive," snivelled Rabeus Farabus. He appeared sad, but optimistic. There was a swoosh sound, and then Viktor Ripmav arrived, finally joining the other three ghosts. He gazed upon Billy and said, "I know you can help Limuria from the brightness that kills it. I used to visit that world, but then it turned too sunny."

"Too sunny?" Billy looked up at Rabeus Farabus and asked.

"Well, Limuria was a very beautiful place. It had no day and no night. It was only an endless twilight—what you call golden hour here on earth," replied Rabeus Farabus.

"Pretty cool," said Segun.

"Please tell me no one else contacted you, have they?" asked Carla Reid, but Segun and Billy's attentions were completely taken by Rabeus Farabus's stories of Limuria. It was only Audrey that had heard what Carla Reid said. She, however, ignored the question. She had grown to like Raco, the lady who helped them escape when they visited Volkodlakea. She didn't see Raco as a threat. In fact, she saw Raco as an ally and therefore, didn't feel the need to tell the ghosts about her. "Through nefarious sorcery and other dastardly acts, many of the beautiful people of Limuria were taken to other worlds. Now Limuria has but a few people enslaved by the Dark One," lamented Rabeus Farabus. He spoke in an animated way by projecting his thoughts on to the air behind him, so that everyone could not only hear what he was talking about, but could also see it. As he spoke, the old Victorian chairs of the Hidden Room, the tables and even the wallpaper vanished until all that appeared behind Rabeus

Farabus was the beautiful world of Limuria in its heyday. "So correct me if I'm wrong, but what you are saying is that the blue-skinned people were all from Limuria?" asked Audrey.

"Clever! Without a doubt, I undoubtedly doubt that you are too clever for you own good, Audrey," replied Arthur Broadbottom with piercing eyes and a slight smirk.

"I bet the princess must have been originally from Limuria,then," commented Segun. "Yes, all the blues were from Limuria... And just like this little black smoke that I am able to conjure. That is how the influence of the Dark One increased over our world until it was but a shadow of its once exuberant past," exclaimed Rabeus Farabus. A tiny black smoke-like substance formed and twirled around his fingers as he dramatised his story so captivatingly well. He floated away from Segun and toward the location of the fourth door, which was still open; ushering the teenagers to go in and rescue the world. Billy was the first to step in, followed by Audrey and finally Segun. Segun was very excited about Limuria because of how Rabeus Farabus described it.

Rabeus Farabus describes Limuria...

However, upon entering the world, they discovered, just as Rabeus Farabus had said, — the world was very sunny instead of the perpetual twilight that it once was. "What are they doing?" asked Segun, looking up at a temple opposite the building that they had just arrived at. "This was a temple dedicated to Estelle," replied Rabeus Farabus, with a sad look on his face. His eyes scanning the building back and forth. "I remember those days. I was king, and I only paid homage to the queen goddess Estelle," he added.

"It looks like they are praying," said Billy.

"Yes, there is an evil entity here that they call Kusnalon. The entity manifested itself because they prayed to it and they keep doing that," commented Rabeus Farabus. "I am now only a ghost, so there is nothing I can do. That is why the three of you are needed here. If you release the moon, it will rise, sending the sun away so that the twilight can return," he added. "So the entity is the sun?" asked Audrey.

"Yes, it is the sun," replied Rabeus Farabus.

"Why did the sun come here in the first place?" asked Billy as they trekked through the ruins of the once great Limuria. They noticed the inhabitants doing nothing but prayer. "The Dark One brought it here," answered Rabeus Farabus. "My time here is over. I must leave you three now. Farewell." His voice resounding as he dematerialised.

"All this talk about the Dark One. Give me a break. Let's just release the stupid moon," said Segun.

"And why would the Dark One bring the sun?" asked Audrey. That time around, even she had questions.

The three teenagers boarded a blue coloured floating train which gave a slight buzzing sound as it rolled through the hills and valleys of Limuria. Their stop was the final one, and they were listening carefully so they didn't miss the stop.

'We are now approaching Moon Land. Please be weary of dark creatures,' said the announcer. The automated train didn't last a minute after reaching Moon Land before it took off. Billy motioned for Segun and Audrey to follow him as they stepped onto the platform. The station was deserted as none of the inhabitants of the dark side of Limuria were interested in travelling to the sunny side. The teenagers observed that the inhabitants of the valley had even bigger eyes than the people from the sunny side of Limuria because they were nocturnal.

"What are we going to do? We can barely see!" bellowed Audrey.

"Relax. Remember the nocturnal spell we learnt?" responded Billy.

"Oh yes, I have it written down," said Audrey. She took out a tiny crumbled up piece of paper from her pocket and repeated the words of the spell. "Sentagoras, sentagoras, oculous noctule," she chanted and Segun followed suit.

"Amazing, I can see a bit clearer, but it's no way near enough," cried Segun.

"Yes, it's only slightly better," Audrey concurred.

"Don't worry, I can see clearly," declared Billy. "come on, follow me. Over there!" Audrey and Segun followed Billy down a steep road further into the valley. The inhabitants of the dark side of Limuria were moving past, going about their business while the teenagers walked along the sidewalks carefully not to attract any unwanted attention. "Alright guys, according to Mr Farabus that should be where the moon is," said Billy, pointing at a tall building with lights on its sides. They walked straight toward the building and on the way, they noticed the inhabitants of the dark side of Limuria engaged in activities, such as playing, singing, and shopping. "Huh? They don't seem so evil," observed Segun.

"Yeah, not at all," replied Audrey.

"Welcome to the moon building. Please move to the right if you are here for a viewing," said a receptionist, who was dressed in a white cloak. He was chaperoning people to queue up on the right-hand side. While other visitors who were there for other purposes were asked to move to the left. There was a huge lift at the centre of the building and other smaller lifts on the sides. "I think the lift in the middle only goes to the penthouse," Billy spoke his thoughts out loud. He gasped and froze for a moment. Why did his thoughts come out as words? He wondered.

"Hmm, that girl is cute. Reminds me of the princess," said Segun.

"Haha, you are still thinking about the princess from Caput Amore?" laughed Audrey. Segun also wondered why he vocalised his thoughts without intending to. He blushed, "I didn't mean to speak out loud. This is so strange," he said. They continued along the queue until they reached the concierge of the moon building.

"Do you have tickets to see the moon?" asked the concierge, a tiny gentleman with a white beard and a crinkled nose. "Huh? Tickets?" replied Billy.

"Oh, you are outsiders. Are you from the sunny part of Limuria?" asked the concierge. Before any of the teenagers could respond, the concierge added, "Everyone, come over here and take a look at people from the sunny side. It's been years since we had anyone come over." The inhabitants of the dark side of Limuria gathered all around the three of them. "Oh hello, what happened to your skin?" asked an old lady.

"Hey look, they are not blue anymore," a man in the crowd bleated.

"We are not from Li—" Segun was about to respond to the questions, but Billy tucked his t-shirt from the side. "They don't need to know we are from Earth," thought Billy, but his words came out. "I didn't mean to say that," he said.

"They can hear our thoughts. Thoughts are not private on

the moon side. I think," commented Audrey. "Haha, of course thoughts are not private," said the concierge as the whole crowd erupted in laughter. "Silence!" a voice came from the lift and the entire crowd was as silent as a graveyard. It was a woman with a crown on her head and a long, flowing dress. She approached the earthlings and while everybody else bowed, Billy was thinking about all the spells he could muster while Segun was looking for the nearest exit, but Audrey was as relaxed as ever and was, in fact, smiling. "Raco?" asked Audrey, looking at the queen as she came closer to them. "Yes, it is me," replied the queen. She motioned for refreshments to be given to her royal guests. "She is the one who helped us in Volkodlakea," said Audrey.

"Yes, we remember her," replied Billy and Segun in unison — relieved.

"Look at the mural on the wall," needled the queen. She pointed at a mural which showed three people on top of a very tall building. "Your arrival has been prophesied. You will free the moon," she carried on. The entire crowd erupted in songs of praise and laughter. The teenagers followed the queen into the central elevator and went straight up for nearly twenty miles, finally reaching the summit. The lift opened into an open space where the moon nestled firmly on top of the building.

"It's beautiful," said Audrey.

"It is indeed. Alright Billy, I don't know how you are going to do it, but everybody has tried, and nobody could ever. So give it a go, will ya," said the queen. "About 800 years ago, the moon fell on the ground for whatever reason and we constructed this building to bring it back as high as we can."

Eleven

Aunt Sarah in Wonderland

"Hello, Sarah... Are you there?" called out Mr Ade over the phone. It was already 2:00 am and Aunt Sarah hadn't returned home. She was supposed to be back since 11 pm. Mr Ade had been trying to get in touch with her, but he's had no joy. She said she'd be working late, but not this late, he thought. "Why are you guys still awake?" he asked. It surprised him to see the boys downstairs. Billy and Segun were at the conservatory near the kitchen. "You must be too hungry to sleep, I guess," he added.

Of course, that was not the reason Billy and Segun had been up, but they pretended as if that were the reason. "Yes, we are so hungry," Billy remarked. He hid the Book of Doors behind the fridge and pretended he was looking for a fork on the floor that had fallen from the nearby dining table. Mr Ade was getting anxious. He had already rung Aunt Sarah over ten times, but her phone's been going straight to voice mail. He was thinking about driving down to her salon to check up on her. Maybe she has some late night customers, he wondered, but even so, she would have called. He glanced at the table and noticed a piece of paper. It was a note scribbled in her handwriting saying she was going to stay at her bestie's place because she was going through 'something' and that she shouldn't be contacted. Why would she write something like that? What was her friend going through? And which of the friends? He knew all of her friends, he thought, but decided to let it be until tomorrow. "Alright boys, make a sandwich and head to bed. It's way past bedtime," he said, and headed back upstairs.

"Is he gone?" whispered Audrey from outside the kitchen window. She'd been hiding in the garden until the coast was clear. "Yeah, come in quietly," answered Segun.

"We don't have to go to the landing to access the Hidden Room," said Billy.

"You mean we can use the other way like the princess used?" asked Audrey.

"Yeah, but Mr Ade might wake up because the house will creak," cautioned Segun.

"Nothing's waking Dad up now—that's for sure. The note I forged in Aunt Sarah's handwriting should do for now," said Billy. They found the entrance from the garden and went straight up the stairs.

Mr Ade searches for Aunt Sarah in the middle of the night...

* * *

Early in the evening, Aunt Sarah actually did return home on time, she noticed Audrey's mobility scooter was parked outside near the front door and not hidden at the back behind the fountain and shrubs where she always hid it when she didn't want anyone knowing she was at the Reid House. That evening, Audrey didn't intend to hide it. In fact, all she wanted to do was give the boys a printout of a map of Azrea she'd been working on and return home, but they decided to travel, briefly.

Aunt Sarah arrived earlier than usual and wanted to surprise the boys with a trip to the movies, but when she saw Audrey's mobility scooter and heard voices upstairs, she knew they were in the Hidden Room. It was at the very moment that they opened one of the doors to go somewhere. She knew she'd heard them up there. She hurriedly went upstairs, but Alfred was barking and snarling at her to stay away from the Hidden Room. Is something wrong? She thought. "Segun! Billy! Where are you?" she screamed. She was getting frustrated with Alfred trying to stop her from accessing the room. "Audrey? I know you are in there. Why are you all keeping quiet?" She was becoming worked up. Alfred bit her long skirt and started pulling her away. He was a pretty big dog, but she was determined to get into the Hidden Room and figure out what was going on in there once and for all. Why were the kids obsessed with that room? They are too old for tree houses and secret rooms, she thought. Luckily, she still had her shoes on, so Alfred couldn't bite her toes off. She thought about giving that dog a kick in the belly. "I will kick you if you don't let me go, Alfred. Do you hear me?" she screamed at Alfred and he backed off as if he'd heard exactly what she had said. Was he afraid? She thought. Alfred suddenly moved away from her and put his head down obediently, as if he were apologising for being such a bad dog. She sighed, and moved the grandfather clock, opening the door to the room, and just as she did, she saw one of the four magical doors still slightly opened and a greenish light emerging from inside. "What the hell? What on earth is that?" she spoke out loud with a puzzled look on her face. Did they jump out through the window? "This isn't even a door. It's literally the wall opening into something," she yelled. So many questions flooded her mind and without further delay she stepped into the unknown. Alfred saw that she had entered and thought he was probably her best hope of survival, so he followed her.

* * *

Moments later, the teenagers returned and noticed that the grandfather clock had moved and the door to the Hidden Room was wide open. Normally, whenever they accessed the room, either Billy or Segun would drag the grandfather clock back in place so that no one suspected that they were inside, but that evening, they knew someone had accessed the room. Audrey returned home to change into something that was more appropriate for travel than her pyjamas, while Segun and Billy went downstairs to look for any signs that could show where Aunt Sarah might have gone to. It was then that Mr Ade went downstairs around 2:00 a.m after waking up and looking over to Aunt Sarah's side of the bed and realising it was still empty.

"I think she might have come home early and heard us talking in the Hidden Room," said Audrey.

"That's impossible. Mum couldn't have travelled," replied Segun. "Could she?"

"There's no other explanation, Segun. We have to find her!" exclaimed Billy. He picked up the planchette and attached the hand of the ballerina. The room vibrated and two doors opened. "That's strange, two doors?" said Segun.

"Yeah, the first one goes to Azrea, and the second goes to Caput Amore," responded Billy.

"Where do we go?" asked Audrey. As the first door started closing.

"Hold it open, Billy," said Segun, "we had just travelled to Azrea earlier when she came into the room, innit?"

"Yes, but earlier, three doors opened at the time. So she could have gone anywhere," replied Billy.

"Oh, we are screwed. Why aren't the ghosts appearing?" asked Audrey. She grabbed the Book of Doors and jumped into the second door just as it began to close. Seeing as she chose to go through the second door, Billy and Segun followed suit.

* * *

They arrived at Caput Amore on a beautiful, warm afternoon. The flowers blossomed and the air smelt of spring. The streets were laid out in cobbled stones and the architecture was otherworldly, with a touch of Romanesque. There were gardens around each city block. "What is that man doing?" asked Audrey as they approached a garden leading to the information centre. "I think he's fixing the garden," replied Segun. The man was hugging a nursery of flowers and strangely enough, the more he embraced the flowers, the more they blossomed. "That's so weird," said Segun.

"I told you guys I've been here before. Put your heads down, no eye contact with anyone or you fall in love with them," responded Billy.

"They keep staring at me," cried Audrey.

"Oh wow, Audrey, you look gorgeous haha," said Segun. He was shocked to see her transform into a tall, beautiful woman. While Billy and Segun turned into young men. "What's happening?" asked Segun.

"I don't know, but I like this body," replied Billy. They reached the centre of Caput Amore and located the information centre. "Guys, I think they have the Looking Glass thing here too, just like in Azrea," said Audrey. She walked faster and entered the building, which had a large crystal in its centre where people asked questions. "So it's like their internet," commented Segun.

"Yup, their internet," responded Billy.

"Okay, show me where my mum is," said Segun. The Large crystal flickered twice and showed Aunt Sarah. "Your mother is in Lower Cremorne. She is working with the resistance," roared the Looking Glass.

"Huh? This one speaks? The one in Azrea didn't speak," marvelled Audrey.

"Tell us more, please. How can we find her? Where is Lower Cremorne?" asked Segun, but the Looking Glass was quiet. "Sorry, speaking times have passed," replied the Looking Glass.

"Don't worry, we'll find her," Billy reassured Segun.

* * *

Later that day, they arrived at Lower Cremorne and found Aunt Sarah at the resistance headquarters. She still looked like herself, but there was something different about her. She was no longer as nervous or worried as she seemed back on Earth. Now she was fearless and ready to pursue her dreams. She had fallen in love with the ideas of the resistance that operated in Caput Amore. "Do you think she will recognise us?" asked Billy.

"Let's see," replied Audrey. They approached Aunt Sarah, who had already made friends.

"Billy, Segun, Audrey. So this is where you come all the time?" she said upon seeing the teenagers.

"No, not only here," replied Audrey.

"Mum, are you okay? Everyone is worried about you," said Segun, perplexed. He had never seen his mother like that. She used to be so reserved, but now so wild. "Yes, I'm okay, son. I have heard everything about the worlds from the resistance. They are working on uniting the worlds," she responded.

"No, you can't be a part of that," Billy challenged her.

"Why dear? We need all the love we can have on Earth," replied Aunt Sarah.

"But that is not what we are supposed to do," remarked Audrey. She turned toward Segun, as if to say persuade your mother. "Mummy, come, we must go back," said Segun.

"Haha, if this is all a dream, then I never want to wake up from it," she replied.

"But what about my dad—Mr Ade? What about us? We are your family," pleaded Billy, but Aunt Sarah was adamant about remaining in Caput Amore. Audrey flipped through the Book of Doors, which she came along with, but there was nothing helpful inside. "I think if we don't take her back, she'll be stuck here forever because she doesn't know the spells," said Audrey.

"I think that's what she wants," replied Billy.

"No!" gasped Segun.

"Boy, am I glad to see the three of you," said a familiar voice from the crowd.

"Oh, it's Alfred!" said Audrey.

"I've always thought that dog was strange," said Aunt Sarah, "so he's human all along."

"That's correct, a human," responded Alfred. He pulled a chair and sat down. "A very handsome human, might I add," he continued. At that moment, Billy recalled the ring that was given to him by his mother, Carla Reid, which had the power to return anyone back to Earth. He pointed it at Aunt Sarah, Alfred,

Segun and Audrey and he wished for them to return. Within a second they vanished and reappeared at the garden near the city block, which they'd entered Caput Amore from earlier.

Before Aunt Sarah realised what was going on, Audrey shoved her through the door and she returned to the Hidden Room. She stood up and immediately tried to return, but there was no door there anymore. It was simply the wooden walls of the old Victorian house. Caput Amore made her fall in love with an idea. The idea of the resistance who sought to unite the worlds. Which was completely against what the ghosts had told the teenagers. She sobbed as she sunk to the floor, still reeling with the romantic idea of the resistance. Mr Ade, who had been up since morning, calling all her friends, heard her sobbing and rushed up to the Hidden Room.

"Sarah, there you are. How did you get in? Are you okay?" he asked.

"I want to go back," she said tearfully.

"Go back where?"

"Through the wall. The kids are there, and the dog. He can talk, he's not a dog. Let's go," she cried.

"What on earth are you talking about? I'm glad you are home safely though," replied Mr Ade happily. He grabbed Aunt Sarah away from the hidden room and thought she was having a nervous break because of stress at work.

Twelve

The Resistance

It had been six weeks since Aunt Sarah's travel to Caput Amore, and things at the Reid House were beginning to settle down. The teenagers still travelled every now and then but were much more cautious than they had been before — so nobody would suspect. Aunt Sarah's memory of Caput Amore rapidly faded and became more of a hazy dream. Mr Ade took her to the hospital, and she was diagnosed with psychotic depression — she was losing touch with reality, according to the doctor.

"You know, Billy, you've never told us what happened at Limuria. How did the moon get back up?" asked Audrey as she dropped her rather heavy bag on the floor. She glanced at Segun but he seemed completely emerged in his video game and didn't care to know how the moon got back up. Billy looked perplexed by Audrey's question. "I don't know," he replied. "I just pressed the red button, and it went back up. There were all these mechanical sounds."

"Red button? But where? We looked everywhere," gasped Audrey.

"Hmm, it was right there," responded Billy.

"Oh, but only you could have seen the button, Billy," said Arthur Broadbottom. His voice emerging from his portrait mounted on the first door.

"Oh, you were here all along?" said Segun.

"Excuse my manners. I just arrived," replied Arthur Broadbottom, who then materialised completely from behind the door. Before long, Carla Reid, Viktor Ripmav and Rabeus Farabus joined him.

"Long time no see," said Billy.

"It came to our knowledge that Aunt Sarah travelled to Caput Amore," commented Arthur Broadbottom with a weary look on his face. "You look tired," Segun said, observing Arthur Broadbottom's ghostly face closely. "We worked tirelessly behind the scenes to make sure your mother returned home safely," replied Arthur Broadbottom.

"Only the young and the pure-hearted can travel safely," said Carla Reid. She floated toward the open window of the Hidden Room. "Travel can be very dangerous if you don't know any spells. Aunt Sarah was very lucky or she would have been lost forever," she added.

"I suspect that she was lured in by the princess of Caput Amore, just like I was deceived once. That is why it is an imperative for you to never allow outsiders back here," said Arthur Broadbottom.

"The Resistance work with the Dark One. They aim to unite the realms. They must be stopped," said Rabeus Farabus.

"The Dark One? I thought he wasn't even human!" exclaimed Segun.

"Precisely. He is evil incarnate, the destroyer of worlds," Rabeus Farabus said, and Viktor Ripmav nodded in agreement. "He was the one who gave the power of evil to Brancanzee in Volkodlakea many years ago. Brancanzee destroyed the scourge of nasty elves, but at serious cost—the curse of vampirism," Viktor Ripmav chimed in.

The ghosts each brought their rich experiences of the Dark One exhaustively while the teenagers listened attentively. They also emphasised time and time again about how and why the Resistance must be stopped. At that moment, Billy thought about how he was enjoying the adventure and how easy it had been for him because of his Reid family-blood. He suddenly had a purpose in his life and he had grown remarkably confident over the last year and a half since they had been in the new house. Segun, on the other hand was more cautious than ever. His experiences while travelling, and especially his mother's travel to Caput Amore, had made him very aware of the danger to all of that. As for Audrey, she cherished the freedom the life of adventure gave her and the knowledge from the experiences that she was gathering. She had now completed the entire maps of all the places they'd travelled to.

"You must now journey to Volkodlakea. Since the last time you had been there, 10 years had passed in that world," said Viktor Ripmav.

"Ten years?" asked a confused Billy.

"Yes, time works slightly differently over there—a lot faster." he replied, his creepy eyes creepier than ever. Billy reassured himself that the ghosts were friendly ghosts and that his mother, Carla Reid, was with them, anyway. "Why do we have to go back to Volkodlakea?" asked Audrey, and Segun suddenly became animated. He wanted to know why, too.

"Well, the vampires have almost been annihilated, except for a few who have created a portal to other worlds. They will now freely travel to earth, and Limuria at will," replied Viktor Ripmav. "Also, I must thank you three. Limuria is now back to the way it was. There is no longer day or night. It is now twilight and beautiful again," Rabeus Farabus said with the look of content in his eyes.

* * *

They arrived at Volkodlakea on a sunny afternoon. The dark smoke used by the vampires to block the light of the sun was no longer floating around in the atmosphere. Brancanzee found a home at Viktor Ripmav's old castle. He was glad to see them and had completely turned his life around. He now taught ferrets how to perform tricks.

"Guys, it says here that every world should have an information centre, like the Looking Glass thingamajig," said Audrey, as she showed Billy and Segun a photo on her phone which she snapped from the Book of Doors. Segun looked at the photo closely and grabbed Audrey's phone. He zoomed in and noticed that on the same page from the Book of Doors —where it was taken from — was a drawing of a man trying to seal off a portal. "Have you seen this, Audrey?" he handed Audrey back her phone.

"Yeah, it's a doodle. Someone who was reading the Book of Doors put it there later," replied Audrey.

"No, it isn't," replied Segun. "It clearly shows a guy get blown to shreds for trying to close a portal. I'm not doing it."

"Ahh, Segun, it's just someone's doodle," Audrey bleated.

"Yes, but it could be true," Segun insisted.

"Alright, Segun, you don't have to stand near the portal—I will. Besides, it's probably not even a portal. Probably just a door," exclaimed Billy. He gave Segun a tap on the back to reassure him that everything would be okay.

A few moments later, they arrived at Brancanzee's house and he confirmed what Viktor Ripmav had said. That the vampires were running away to other worlds through portals. Audrey's heart sunk after hearing that. She thought about her mother, who saw ghosts a few times and hadn't been the same ever since. "They want us to seal the portals. I don't think we should," said Segun.

"Of course we must," Billy turned around to remonstrate with Segun.

"But the Book of Doors says the portals must be maintained," replied Segun.

"It's a doodle! Jeez Segun," exclaimed Audrey. She didn't understand why Segun was behaving that way, and neither did Billy. Upon seeing how determined Billy and Audrey were about closing the portals, Segun reclined his position and agreed to help. Brancanzee led them to the secret location of the Resistance, who were aiding the vampires to escape. "We have to convince them to stop helping vampires," thundered Audrey as they entered the hideout. It was an inconspicuous location atop a hill, surrounded by a moat that had alligators.

"Please, stop helping vampires. We are here to seal the portals," yelled Billy, with his chest up high as he barged in. Some of the vampires glanced at Billy when he stormed in. Some were seated by a dried up blood bar while others were scurrying all over the place like deranged insomniacs.

"Not a chance," said the princess from Caput Amore. "The portals must be left open and anyone is free to travel to other worlds, vampire or not," she added. Audrey surreptitiously glanced at Billy, who shook his head in disagreement. "No, we are here to seal the portals," said Billy. Inside the secret hideout of the resistance was a door that the vampires were using to escape Volkodlakea, just as Billy thought it might be. Some of the vampires were exhausted from prolonged lack of blood and proper rests — Volkodlakea was no longer their world. "Listen to me, there are many worlds that they can go to. Even vampire worlds who manufacture synthetic blood for food. They are not all killers," yelled the princess. "Continue letting them through!" she ordered.

"You'll have to stop us first," declared Audrey. "*Ignis impetum*," she chanted and a fireball about the size of an apple was hurled toward Princess Mabila. However, something strange happened to the fireball. As it grew closer to Princess Mabila, it simply disappeared. "Your little fireballs spells will not harm me, Audrey," said the princess.

"Huh? How is this possible?" cried Billy.

"I simply have too much love around me," said Princess

Mabila. "Now, get out of my way," she added and gracefully trotted off, but Audrey wasn't done.

"Come on guys, let's chant together, *ignis impetum*," Audrey chanted again and soon after Billy was chanting with her, but Segun was still not taking part. The fireballs grew larger and faster with each attempt, but still didn't cause the princess any visible harm. However, the fireballs were hitting the walls of the old fort-tuned hideout and also hitting the vampires and other members of the Resistance. "Billy, Audrey, stop you are harming people," screamed Princess Mabila, who appeared to crouch and pick up a bag of water to clean herself. "Look, she is dowsing herself with some sort of magical water," huffed Audrey, pointing at the bag of water.

"It's water from the fountain in our garden back at home," exasperated Segun. "The two of you need to stop this.".

"He's right, Audrey," said Billy.

"Well, it's about time. You don't have to do everything you read in some book, you know," Princess Mabila exulted. She pulled out one of the chairs arranged around a table and sat down in the middle of the room. Seeing as the coast was clear, the vampires started leaving again. One by one, the long queue of vampires was getting smaller and smaller. "Are you okay?" Segun asked the princess.

"I'll be okay. Luckily, I had enough of the fountain water," she replied wearily.

"Look, we are sorry, I guess," said Billy.

"We didn't know the vampires were going to their world," Audrey chimed in. Segun pulled out a chair and sat next to the princess and Billy thought how much taller than them the princess was. If they didn't know any spells, they couldn't have had a snowball's chance in hell.

"So, what exactly is the Resistance?" asked Segun. Princess Mabila, who had her head down to catch her breath, looked up at them with her large eyes. She said, "We aid in the movement of people around the worlds."

"Is that all?" asked Billy.

"Talk about inter-dimensional emigration, ha," joked Segun. The princess smiled and replied to Billy's question, "Yes, that's all we do."

"So, you don't work with the Dark One?" asked Audrey.

"No one has ever seen the Dark One," replied Princess Mabila.

"But we were told that the Resistance work with the Dark One," said Audrey, growing more confused by the minute. "Who told you that?" asked Princess Mabila. Audrey wanted to speak but didn't quite trust the princess, so she didn't say a word. The princess realised Audrey didn't trust her. Her eyebrows were raised and arched. She looked at Billy, who was still standing, and then at Segun, who was seated near her. Segun said "We were told by the ghosts who live in our house."

The princess burst out laughing, "You are having ghosts problems then, haha. Take this stone when the three of you want to speak in private. They won't be able to hear you," she yawned, handing over the stone to Segun: a red crystal wrapped in leather.

"Look, all the vampires have left," pointed out Audrey.

"Nothing to snivel about. They are in their world," responded Princess Mabila. She stood up, made her way to the door and bade the teenagers goodbye as she leapt in.

Thirteen

Earth's Looking Glass

"What exactly is a year ten student like me doing halfway across the world, over 200 feet above sea level in some Mexican forest?" screamed Segun as he squinted at the foggy forest below while precariously hanging on a gigantic Amazonian tree branch. "That's a question, I wish I had an answer for," yelled back Audrey who was also hanging on a branch not too far from Segun. "Wait a minute, where's Billy?" she added.

"Over here!" yelled Billy. He was slightly luckier than Audrey and Segun as he was over fifty feet below them on a less complicated tree. Earlier that day, they had attempted to use a portal which would have transported them to Earth's looking glass.

"Guys, Brancanzee's potion!" screamed Audrey. After recalling one of the purposes of using items from other worlds. "Drink your potions. It says so in the Book of Doors!" she hollered. They each used the vial of Brancanzee's potion, that they had in their pockets. "Nothing's happening. I'm still here," shrieked Segun. Who was still hanging up there.

"Give it some time," replied Audrey. Soon after, they disappeared from that predicament and reappeared on the ground. "So why didn't it work the first time?" said Billy in jest as he picked out pieces of broken shrubs from his shoes.

"Beats me," replied Audrey.

"Well at least it got us close enough," responded Billy.

"Close enough to the jaws of a jaguar, that's for sure," huffed Segun.

"There was a jaguar?" shrieked Audrey.

"There's always a jaguar," replied Segun.

* * *

They arrived at the foothills of a gigantic structure. It was a huge mound covered with earth and trees. Audrey read from the Book of Doors: "*When you arrive at the destination, bear in mind that the sands of time would likely have obscured its very structure. So, you will not know how ingress is to be done but fret not, for repeat this spell and the very walls will move to make way for you.*" The three of them chanted "*Pulchra aggeribus vel terram movere tur ut fiat,*" and eventually an entrance opened and they went down inside the mound as it closed behind them and magical lights illuminated the interior. "Look! It's the looking glass thingamajig," pointed Audrey.

"Yup, it sure is," replied Billy.

"So remind me why we are here again?" asked Segun.

"Did our trip make you lose a screw, Segun?" replied Audrey.

"Broadbottom said we have to find all the looking glasses of the four worlds," said Billy.

"Yes, I know, but what are we going to do with the stupid looking glass? It's impossible to carry one of those," replied Segun.

"Behold, it's there," said Billy. He felt triumphant as he arched his back to go under a fallen megalithic block.

"Oh, thank goodness," said Audrey, who was trying to catch up with the boys. It wasn't easy for her because without her mobility scooter, she had to use a walking stick and even so, she was slow, but she never complained. She savoured every moment. Segun ran past Billy and went straight to the looking glass. "Looking glass, where is our house?" he asked, but Earth's looking glass was unresponsive. "It didn't work," he yelled toward Billy and Audrey, who were still only just catching up. "Well, keep trying," said Audrey.

"Looking glass, where is my mother?" he asked again, but the looking glass was just a dusty, rectangular-crystalline mass on the ground. "So, I guess it's not working," said Billy. He placed his hands on the surface of the large stone as soon as he reached the looking glass, but nothing happened. "Oh, all this trip for nothing," grumbled Audrey. "Why us?"

"Who made these things anyway?" asked Segun as he sat down on the ground with his back resting against the looking glass. "I don't know, some ancient person with nothing better to do," replied Audrey.

"Wait a minute. It's pretty much like the internet, right?" asked Billy. His eyes lit up with the idea brewing in his mind. "If it's like the internet then, this crystal is just the display, the interface," he added.

"Yeah, so?" asked Segun.

"Well, maybe we can reset it or connect it with our phones?"

"Huh? How?" asked Audrey.

"I don't know, think," replied Billy. They looked and looked around the ancient underground temple, but there was no way of resetting the looking glass. They'd already been in there for over an hour and Segun was already starving, while Audrey was getting tired and upset. It was then that Billy's idea finally took form. He picked up the Book of Doors and handed it over to Segun telling him to hold it firmly on one side of the looking glass, while he stood on the opposite side and shined the torch of his phone through the looking glass, directed at the Book of Doors. The Looking glass then lit up briefly and cast an inverted image of the Book of Doors around the room.

"Aha! it works with light," said Audrey.

"Whoa, crazy tho," said Segun.

"But how are we going to light this place up?" lamented a perplexed Billy with his hand on his chin and his eyes staring at empty space. "Hey snap out of it. Look here," Audrey pointed at a lever and Segun tried to move the lever but he couldn't. In the middle of all that, Billy noticed a mark on the giant crystal. It was the letter 'R' carved into the looking glass. Billy then remembered the ring that was given to him by his mother, Carla Reid. He placed the ring on top of the crystal and it lit up. "It's working haha, wow," rejoiced Segun and Audrey's smile was ear to ear.

"This is amazing. We found Earth's looking glass," she said.

"Where is my mother?" said Segun, and the surroundings of the shop was displayed. Aunt Sarah was at her shop attending to customers. "Where is Daddy?" asked Billy and Mr Ade was seen washing his face in the toilet of a large shopping mall where he worked part time as a security officer. "Huh? Why is he always in a toilet?" asked Audrey, and the three of them burst out laughing. "Where can I find a million pounds?" asked Segun and the looking glass displayed the vault of a bank with about a million pounds. "Don't be silly, Segun. Ask something important," whined Audrey.

"You are one to complain haha," replied Segun.

"Okay, I have a serious question. Where is Princess Mabila?

You know, the one Segun likes?" joked Billy, while trying his hardest to keep a straight face.

"I don't like her, just said she was fit, innit," replied Segun.

"Ew, that blue skin," cringed Audrey.

"Okay, okay, serious question now. How can the Dark One be defeated?" asked Billy, but the looking glass just flickered on and off.

"Huh?" gasped Audrey.

"Tell us how!" Billy asked the looking glass again, but nothing happened.

"Show us the Dark One, then," asked Segun, but the looking glass did not respond. The 'magical' lights that had turned on when they arrived at the mound suddenly flickered. "I think we are no longer welcome here!" yelled Audrey. "Let's leave." They made their way back to the entrance but it was sealed just like it had been when they arrived. "Let's try the spell again," said Segun.

"*Pulchra aggeribus vel terram movere tur ut fiat,*" they chanted in unison, but nothing happened. Audrey began to panic while Segun's eyes characteristically grew larger, while droplets of sweat appeared on the sides of his face.

"We are trapped!" he worried.

"Relax, all we need to do is to ask the looking glass," replied Billy. He calmly walked toward the large crystal and asked. The looking glass displayed a wooden door with metallic hinges and around it—stone blocks.

"Wait up guys, I've seen that door on the way down here," said Audrey as she tried to keep up.

They left the looking glass and made their way toward the

direction of the door—led by Audrey. Segun opened the door, but it just led to a little cellar and there was nothing inside. "Could it be a door that can send us back home?" asked Segun, "you guys wait here, I'll run back to the looking glass and ask how the door works." He ran back to the looking glass but the device only displayed 4:00 P.M, no matter how many times Segun asked. He looked at his phone and it was five minutes to four. That must mean the door only works at 4:00 P.M, he thought.

"Lets wait until 4:00 PM," he said and at exactly 4:00 P.M, they opened the door, but nothing happened. By then, the look of worry was beginning to show even on Billy's face. "Oh my God, what do we do?" said Audrey, but no one replied. Instead, Billy rushed back to looking glass. "Who made the looking glass?" he asked. Segun and Audrey were not too far behind Billy when he asked the question. They glanced at each other and wondered what an odd question to ask in the situation they were in. The looking glass displayed a hooded figure. "Who made all the looking glasses?" asked Audrey and the looking glass displayed the image of men and women labouring to put the device together. That doesn't help their situation much, though, thought Segun.

"Show us the looking glass in the kingdom of Azrea," said Segun, and the beautiful kingdom of Azrea was shown but their looking glass had been destroyed. "Okay guys, we really need to get out of here," said Audrey.

"Wait a minute. I think that is why Broadbottom wanted us to find the looking glass. They are being destroyed," exclaimed Billy. He had that triumphant look on his face again, as if he had it all figured out. "Look, I think the crystal is cracking," observed

Segun. "let's move back a little." As they stepped away from the crystal, it cracked even more.

"Billy, my son," came a rather faint voice from the room that they were directed to by the looking glass.

"Over there, it's Billy's mother," pointed Segun and they walked toward the cellar door.

"Boy, am I glad to see her," said Audrey.

"Mother, how can we get out of here?"

"This door is not like the ones in the Hidden Room. It is very dangerous to use. When I learnt that the entrance was blocked, I knew I had to come here to get the three of you home safely," answered Carla Reid. She appeared like a radiant light offering to help them in such a dire situation. Before long, Arthur Broadbottom also appeared. "This door is the only exit from this hellhole. Unfortunately, we can't determine where you are going to go if you use the door. The door is also a conduit for nefarious sprites," said Arthur Broadbottom. The teenagers were so glad to see the ghosts that they had been so accustomed to over the last couple of months.

"Sprites? What are those?" shrieked a berserk Segun.

"They are spirits of wicked elves. When they die, they turn to sprites and they use this door," replied Carla Reid. An idea ran through Billy's mind. He pointed his magical ring at Audrey and Segun and wished them to return to the Hidden Room, but it didn't work. "The ring isn't goin to work on Earth, my son," said Carla Reid.

"Oh no!" said Billy. The door of the underground cellar began to vibrate and the sprites came rushing through. Their bright bodies illuminated the whole underground enclosure, revealing beautiful wall arts that surrounded the looking glass. The beings made no notice of the teenagers and went straight to the looking glass. "What are they doing?" asked Audrey.

"I think they are trying to fix it," replied Segun.

"Try as they may, they will not be able to fix it," monotoned Arthur Broadbottom.

"But why?" asked Segun. The sprites emitted a rather loud and disturbing buzzing sound. "Come on, my lovelies. This way!" yelled Carla Reid, swinging her ghostly arm in the direction of the door. "If you leave now before the door is closed again, you can make it somewhere safe," she directed. Broadbottom floated toward the door while the sprites were still oozing out and heading straight for the looking glass like bees to nectar. He turned to Segun and said, "Well, to answer your question, young man, the sprites can't mend anything on earth. They are wasting their time — those mindless vagabonds." Audrey was the first to reach the door of the cellar, followed by Billy and finally Segun, who had stayed behind, feeding his curious eyes with the seemingly mindless sprites floating about. They reminded him of tropical insects that come out of nowhere after rain and then die when the sun comes up. He had seen such insects on a trip with his mother.

"We'll have to leave you here. Godspeed, go now before the portal closes," said Carla Reid. The teenagers went through the door to the cellar, now transformed into a twirling portal. "I'm so glad Broadbottom and Carla showed up," said Audrey, as her voice trailed into oblivion.

Fourteen

The God of the Sprites

It seemed like forever, since they'd stepped into the cellar door, but they were still floating in what appeared like a void-space. They were used to travelling to the four worlds closest to Earth which share most of Earth's physics. However, this time around, they were somewhere completely different. The air was soothing, calm and fragrant, but the world itself—wherever it was—was too bright to see. So, they had their hands placed tightly over their eyes. No one dared to take a glimpse of the world they had just arrived in. "Is there any spell for this Audrey?" asked Segun, as he sunk comfortably in a suede-like cushion. "I can see. I can see now," said Billy.

"Why is that? You can always see when we can't?" replied Audrey.

"H...How?" stammered Segun.

"I don't know. I can just see," said Billy. Audrey put her

hands inside her pocket to see if she had the little piece of paper where she had written the seeing spell but she couldn't find it. "I remember the seeing spell," yelled Segun, "*Sentagoras, sentagoras, oculous noctule,*" he chanted loudly and jubilated as his vision cleared, which prompted Audrey to do the same.

"Oh my god, sprites everywhere!" shouted Audrey.

"So this is the world of the sprites," commented Segun as he looked up at a pillar of light which seemed infinitely high. The sprite's white bodies floated high up, trying to reach the top of the pillar and their dragonfly-like wings flapping and buzzing. "Broadbottom said they were evil, right?" asked Segun.

"Yeah, so let's hurry and find a way back home," replied Billy, and Audrey nodded in agreement. They walked through the world of the sprites which was nothing like they'd imagined it could be if there ever were such a place. The ground was so soft and made up of a material with the same texture as suede, while the grass was as soft as cotton and golden in colour. "If this is a world like all the others, surely we should be able to find its looking glass thing, right?" said Audrey.

"Yes, good idea," replied Segun and Billy in unison.

"Let's ask someone or something," said Segun.

"A sprite? They aren't even looking at us," responded Audrey.

"Hey, can you hear us? Hey, we need help to get home," said Billy, trying to get the attention of a sprite, but the sprite flapped his wings away as if he hadn't heard Billy. Segun took a small rock on the floor and was about to throw it at a passing sprite when someone held his hand from behind. "Stop that, Segun. We should be glad to be here," said Mr Ade. He was standing behind the three of them with such a crazy but happy expression on his face. "What? Dad? How did you get here?" gasped Billy. His father was the last person he was expecting to see in any of the worlds, let alone the world of sprites. "What makes you think you are the only one that can come here, Billy?" replied Mr Ade. He squatted down for about half a second and then he sprang up like a spring and flew away in the air with the sprites. "Just call me if you need me," he said, as he got farther and farther away.

"That was so strange," said Audrey, who had been quiet the whole time.

"Okay, he was acting mad-funny," said Segun.

"So, first Aunt Sarah, now this?" said Billy. "We've got to find him and take him back home," he added.

* * *

The farther away they got from the pillar of light at the centre of the world of the sprites the darker and scarier the world became. Perhaps Arthur Broadbottom was right, thought Audrey — the sprites must have been elves before. She noticed that there were street names and other road signs written in elven alphabets. She also saw old statues of elves that were clearly not made by the sprites. "Maybe this world is the ghost of the world of the elves," she said.

"You've noticed the same thing, haven't you?" said Billy.

"What are you guys on about?" asked Segun. All he saw was a scary world growing darker and darker, the farther away from the pillar of light they got. "I think we are in Volkodlakea," concluded Audrey.

"Yes, you are right. Look, this road should lead to Viktor Ripmav's castle," pointed out Billy.

"Okay, you guys have completely lost me. There is no way this is Volkodlakea," said Segun. "It looks like it, but not it." Billy took the lead as if he was looking for something at Viktor Ripmav's castle. Audrey caught up with him while Segun was standing there looking at the two of them before deciding to follow along. Indeed, the world of the sprites was the ghost of other worlds. The elves that had died at Volkodlakea during the wars with the humans had brought a piece of Volkodlakea to the afterlife.

"I was right. It's Viktor Ripmav's castle," said Billy.

"Should we go in?" asked Audrey.

"It's so dark," said Segun. They entered the castle from its lower ground floor where Viktor Ripmav's secret laboratory was in the real Volkodlakea but over in the world of the sprites, they did not see the lab. Instead, it was just a large open area — a dungeon of sorts. They used the lift, which worked by adding water to a bucket attached to a system of pulleys, just as it was in Volkodlakea. Audrey was marvelling at the similarity while Billy was focused on reaching Viktor Ripmav's room so he could find the door in the closet that they used to leave Volkodlakea in the real Volkodlakea. Segun, on the other-hand, was thinking something was amiss. "If this is a copy of Volkodlakea, or some kind of memory of it, brought here by the elves, why would they bring a vampire's house?" he asked.

"I think they just brought over their old world," replied Audrey.

"Yes, but doesn't make sense. Why bring anything that would

remind them of their enemies?" asked Segun, but Audrey's attention was focused elsewhere.

"Over here! This is the closet!" yelled Billy. He had already found the door that led back to the Hidden Room in the real Volkodlakea but unfortunately, it was useless there. He opened the door but it didn't lead to the Hidden Room. "We are screwed," said Segun.

"Mr Ade!" screamed Audrey, "Mr Ade!"

"Daddy, come if you can hear us!"

"He did say we should call him if we needed help, innit," commented Segun, "but can he hear us? Would be dope if he could." Within a second, Mr Ade arrived.

"You need help getting out of this world, don't you?" he asked.

"Yes, and how did you get here?" asked Billy.

"You keep asking that question. Listen, just do what you need to do. Go and get a job from the pillar of light, finish the job, get paid and go back," he replied.

"Huh? Get a job? I don't even have a job even on Earth," said Segun.

"You boys keep acting like you don't know how to live. We do this every night. We just don't remember when we wake up," said Mr Ade. He walked to the corner of the replica of Viktor Ripmav's large bedroom and drew open the heavy, thick curtains; revealing a large arched window which he flew out of.

"Wow, I think Daddy is sleeping," said Billy.

"Yeah, he didn't come here from the Hidden Room," responded Audrey.

"He's heading toward the tower of light, just like the sprites," said Billy.

"If you look carefully, you'll see that Mr Ade isn't the only human here. There are a few humans flying around together with the sprites too," observed Segun.

"Yes, that's true. Let's fly to the tower of light then," said Billy.

* * *

They flew high over the ghost town and observed all the places that they knew in the real Volkodlakea— Brancanzee's old castle and the central library were some of the biggest structures. The tower of light was intricately designed with ornaments such as pearls and other precious stones. The sprites were going in to get jobs and then venture out into the dark city to carry out those tasks — just as Mr Ade had said. "So that is what Mr Ade was talking about," said Audrey as she pointed at a sprite reading a letter he had just received and getting ready to carry out the contents of the letter. "There are some humans also reading the letters," said Billy.

"So the sprites were too busy to even notice us," said Segun.

"Of course, young man. Nobody has time to waste. We come here for our daily jobs and have it done as soon as possible. No complaints," said a sprite that was standing in the queue, inside the tower of light — waiting to receive his letter.

"Huh? you can speak?" asked Segun.

"Well, of course, we are not mindless you know, just busy." replied the sprite. By then Billy, who was ahead of Segun and Audrey in the queue had already reached the till. "Sorry, no humans here. Go upstairs to receive a human job," said the sprite at the till. Billy left the queue and motioned for Audrey and Segun to follow him upstairs. There was a lift that went to the top of the tower of light that apparently the sprites never went up to. "Come on, let's just take the lift," said Audrey, and Segun nodded in agreement. There were only two buttons in the lift. Both of which had the letter G on them. "I guess this button down here means ground floor, right?" asked Audrey.

"Yes, it has to be," said Billy.

"So what's the other 'G' then, God?" joked Segun. He pressed the button and the transparent lift went straight up while the sprites looked up on every floor as the lift zoomed higher and higher. The top floor was mostly empty — there were absolutely no sprites. The teenagers wandered through the very luxurious top floor, going through room after room until they finally heard voices. It was Mr Ade having tea with a lady who had her back turned towards them. On seeing them, he said, "Oh, great to see you've made it. I'm very proud of you three."

"Please, come, and have some tea. You must be tired," said the lady as she turned towards them.

"Raco?" said Audrey.

"Aha, you know her," said Mr Ade, "but of course, you must," he added.

"She's helped us escape at Volkodlakea," said Segun.

"Aha," acknowledged Mr Ade.

"So, where do we get a job?" asked Billy.

"Over there at the looking glass. The job is mostly to develop your spirit. You don't have to, but it's very good," replied Mr Ade.

"Where is the looking glass?" asked Billy.

"Its upstairs," replied Mr Ade. They walked out and saw the looking glass on top of the building, and attached to it were tubes that went all the way down to the other levels of the sky-scraper. "Look, the letters are coming from here," observed Billy. "That's correct," said Raco.

"Wait a minute, you are the hooded figure," observed Billy. He recalled that Earth's looking glass displayed the image of a hooded figure when asked who created the looking glass. "Who are you?" asked Segun.

"I am a traveler like you. I am not sleeping and I am not dreaming. The looking glass helps us know where we are," replied Raco.

"We want to go back home," said Audrey.

"Of course, my dear Audrey. I've helped you before and I shall help you again. The fifth door through that corridor on the left will take you back to your world," responded Raco.

"Hmm, so this tower of light is the God of the sprites," concluded Segun.

Fifteen

Return to the Kingdom of Azrea

"Wake up, boys. Today is the day we are going to the museum," said Aunt Sarah, barging into Billy's room. Segun's room was right opposite Billy's and from the looks of things, she was there first. Billy rolled back in bed even though he had heard her. It was one of those days where he just didn't feel like getting out of bed. He hardly had any sleep last night because of nightmares. "Billy isn't waking up," complained Aunt Sarah. She made her way downstairs and Mr Ade who was already downstairs, could be heard saying, "Oh, must be puberty. I remember those days. You just don't wanna get out of bed." Segun heard and started laughing. "Billy is way past puberty. He's almost fifteen," yelled Aunt Sarah.

"No babe, puberty in boys is anywhere between 9 and 15. So he's a late bloomer, maybe."

"It's nothing to do with that. I just have a headache. Couldn't sleep last night," exclaimed Billy. He had finally come downstairs but was still in his pyjamas — a hoodie. "Aren't you guys going to call Audrey?" asked Mr Ade.

"Audrey is a girl. I'm sure she has girlfriends she'd rather hang out with on a Saturday. They are too old for those hidden room board games now. I bet she now has—," replied Aunt Sarah.

"Hey everyone, time for the museum, right?" interjected Audrey, as she barged into the Reid House. "Audrey, I was just asking them if they'd told you," said Aunt Sarah. Mr Ade had started to doze off on the couch. "Argh, sleeping again?" complained Aunt Sarah. Billy, who was also sleepy, glanced at his father and said, "Were you having dreams?" Audrey and Segun knew what Billy was referring to. They'd seen Mr Ade in the world of the sprites, but he clearly didn't remember. "Dreams? Nah, I don't think so," replied Mr Ade. He yawned and made his way toward the TV and picked up his car keys. "You do dream sometimes. Last night you said sprite. I thought you were thirsty, but sprite? Think about something healthier next time, hun," commented Aunt Sarah.

* * *

At the museum, Segun noticed a section about the local history and wondered if there was anything on Stony Oak, but he couldn't find much. "Nothing in boring old Stony Oak, Segun," said Billy.

"Yeah, ditto to that," agreed Audrey. Aunt Sarah had never

been a fan of museums, and she secretly intended to go to the nearby spa. That was the only reason she'd suggested an outing that far away from home.

"Over there, it's a ghost tour. Do you guys want to see it?" asked Mr Ade, pointing toward a small group. "No, I pass," said Aunt Sarah. Mr Ade chuckled, knowing she was scared of anything with the word 'ghost' in it. He thought maybe he shouldn't have mentioned that in the first place, given her recent bout with hysteria after accidentally travelling to Caput Amore; although he didn't know exactly what happened to her. She didn't seem hysterical to him anymore. "Okay, everyone, how about we meet here at 12:00 PM and go back home," he said and everybody agreed. Billy joined the ghost tour and so did Audrey, but Segun wandered off somewhere else. "There is a famous ghost that moves around this street. It is said that he was the son of an earl that once lived here," said the ghost tour guide. That's exciting, thought Audrey.

"Could he be the son of Arthur Broadbottom?" Billy asked.

"Well, maybe," replied Audrey as they continued to learn about other ghosts that supposedly haunted the streets at night.

Meanwhile, Segun was walking down the alleys of the old town centre on his own when he heard someone say, "He's not my real father. The earl is lying."

"Huh?" gasped Segun, "who said that?"

"I did. I'm right here," the voice replied. It was coming from a dusty window, but there was no one inside the small cabin. It must be a ghost, thought Segun. He went looking for Audrey and Billy. "I heard a ghost," he said as he interrupted the very exciting ghost tour, which included everything except any real ghosts. "Where?" replied Billy.

"Come here," said Segun, "the ghost said he's not my real father. He's referring to the earl of Stony Oak."

"Haha, lies," said the ghost tour guide, but the people seemed more interested in what Segun had to say than the ghost tour, so they all followed Segun. "Wait, come back," screamed the tour guide.

Down at the alley, an old lady reported that she'd heard the ghost too and another, but no one could see the ghost except for Billy. "Tell me your name," said Billy.

"I am Faraday Broadbottom," replied the ghost.

"So Arthur Broadbottom is your father?" asked Billy.

"Yes, but he was killed by a man who looked just like him. The real Arthur Broadbottom is not still in the Reid House," replied the ghost.

"Huh? That is so confusing," said Billy.

"You must go to Azrea," instructed the ghost.

***

Later that day, they arrived at the kingdom of Azrea and noticed that the streets and houses were not as beautiful as they once were. "What happened here?" asked Segun.

"Look, there's rubble everywhere," said Audrey.

"Usually, they fix it up when the dark one leaves, don't they?" asked Segun.

"Yes, something's wrong," agreed Billy. They reached the centre of Azrea and noticed that the looking glass had been destroyed. "Welcome back, travellers. Our crystal, it's gone,"

"What could have done such a thing?" asked Segun.

"It's Arthur Broadbottom," said Billy.

"Yes, didn't they say we needed to destroy all the looking glasses?" said Audrey.

"They did, but why? Looking glasses are gods, remember?" said Segun.

"How are they gods?" asked Audrey.

"In the worlds of the sprites, that's literally their god," responded Segun.

"Just because they get jobs there or whatever, doesn't make it their god," said Audrey, "besides, Broadbottom said the Dark One gets his power from the looking glass."

"But Broadbottom could be wrong. Remember what Faraday Broadbottom said?" protested Segun.

"Stop arguing Segun. How do you know?" asked Audrey.

"I don't know, but it could be," he insisted.

"Okay, guys. Let's just go back to the Hidden Room and find out what's going on," said Billy.

* * *

At the Hidden Room, Carla Reid was already seated quietly when they arrived. "Hello Mum," said Billy.

"Good to see you," she replied.

"The looking glass in Azrea has been destroyed," said Billy.

"Yes, that is for the best," replied Carla Reid.

"I told you guys," said Audrey.

"So if that's the case, why are they suffering in Azrea? They can't build their houses back as fast as they used to. Seems to me like the looking glass isn't evil — it helps them," said Segun.

"No, the looking glasses were made by the Dark One, Segun," replied Carla Reid. "It's the all-seeing eye of the Dark One. That's how he controls people across the worlds," replied Carla Reid.

"Is Broadbottom an imposter?" asked Billy.

"An imposter? I'll rather call him to answer that question himself. What I do know, is that I've known him since I was a little girl," replied Carla Reid. She floated toward the first door and knocked three times, and Arthur Broadbottom replied with a knock. Before long, the knob turned, and he entered the room. "I see you have met Faraday Broadbottom." he said.

Billy nodded and answered, "Yes, I saw him. He said you are not his real father."

"That is correct. I am his stepfather. The Dark One has got a firm hold of that one," responded Arthur Broadbottom.

"Please do not trust anyone on this very important journey you are undertaking for humanity. You are part of something great. All of you," said Carla Reid. Her comments were reassuring enough for Audrey. Billy still wasn't sure, but Segun was convinced that the looking glasses were gods. "Are looking glasses, gods?" he asked.

"I thought you were a man of science, Segun. They are just communication devices, but now the Dark One is channelling his influence through them all," replied Arthur Broadbottom.

"So, like corrupting the internet, hmm," commented Billy. Segun reached inside his pocket and felt the crystal given to him by the princess and brought it out of his pocket. He placed it on the centre table in the Hidden Room and Carla Reid and Broadbottom felt a feeling of discomfort all over their ghostly bodies —making them disappear. "So, it works," he said. "Remember the princess said it helps against ghost problems. I should have used it on that Faraday Broadbottom guy."

However, Billy had another idea. "Give me the crystal, Segun. How about we carry out an investigation without the four ghosts ever finding out? Since they are allergic to this thing," he said.

"That makes sense. Let's be objective," replied Segun.

"What? You guys are giving the Dark one a chance? Seriously? That's like the Devil, right?" Audrey was berserk. "Count me out," she said and left the Hidden Room.

"Audrey, wait," said Segun.

"Relax, she'll come around," replied Billy.

* * *

Later in the evening, Billy and Segun had begun their investigations. They planned to travel to all four worlds to find out what was really going on, and Alfred seemed so determined to travel with them. "You know what, boys? I'm glad you got that crystal from that fine princess," said Alfred. He was a talking dog again in Azrea. "Oh yeah, why is that?" asked Segun.

"Well, I've always liked Billy's mother since I was little. When she died, I got stuck in that world with her until Billy found us, but that Broadbottom guy I was never sure about," replied Alfred.

"Oh, really?" responded Segun.

"Oh, for sure, and don't even get me started on that vampire and the other weirdo," he said.

Billy noticed that the magical creatures in Azrea had started running away into their houses and the beautiful sunny weather was about to turn dark as they approached the king's castle, where he was hoping to get some answers. The king was seated on his throne but as it was getting darker, he too was on his way indoors. "Whenever the Dark One comes, they turn into hideous creatures," said Alfred.

"But we are here to investigate. So we will not hide," replied Billy. Very soon the sky grew darker and darker and those who had not yet left for thier houses completely transformed into hideous creatures and began to tear up the whole place. It was pandemonium, but Billy didn't care. He tried the flying spell to go all the way up, but he couldn't see anything. "Come back, Billy, I have an idea," yelled Alfred. "What is it?" asked Billy.

"Because I'm a dog, I can transform into something that can fly up higher," replied Alfred.

"Great, let's do it. Go up and see what's causing the darkness," said Billy. Alfred, transformed into a large bird. "This is called the thunderbird," he said. "Hop on." Billy and Segun sat on Alfred's back and he soared higher and higher, but they still couldn't see the source of the darkness. "Can you transform into anything bigger?" asked Segun.

"No, I can't. Never could," replied Alfred as he gently glided back down to the courtyard of the king's castle, which was now just rubble after all the carnage that was going on.

"Yes, you can transform into something much bigger," said Audrey, who was waiting for them down on the grounds of the courtyard. "Audrey? You came," said Segun.

"Yes, I couldn't let you guys just go alone and mess up," she replied.

"*Convertere ad draconem*," said Audrey, and Alfred grew scales. His hind legs grew bigger than that of fifty elephants and, within a short amount of time, he turned into a luminous green dragon. "Audrey, I didn't know you knew that spell. I'ts not even in the Book of Doors," said Billy.

"The Book of Doors doesn't know everything," she said and Segun smiled. She finally believes what he's been saying all along, he thought. "Hop on then, let's go," said Alfred, but Segun assumed a body posture that implied he wasn't going to get on Alfred's large scaly back and Audrey shook her head from right to left, showing she wasn't going. So, the task fell squarely on Billy's shoulders. Alfred, now a humongous dragon, roared and jumped so high. He was perhaps as high as a forty-storey building just from his initial jump. Even before he began to flap his wings, he disappeared from their range of view within a matter of seconds. Alfred was so massive that he was bigger than a blue whale and Billy had to think of all the spells he knew that could keep him from falling off Alfred's back.

At a tremendous height of about 40,000 feet above sea level, Billy noticed something moving up there. It must be the Dark One, he thought, but it was too massive for him to see what it was. If they fly any higher, neither he nor Alfred would be able to breathe as that would be outer space. "Alfred, go back!" shouted Billy. Whatever that black thing was, it was in outer space, thought Billy. "Okay, I'm heading back down," roared Alfred. He then descended back down to the king's courtyard.

Sixteen

A Meeting with the Dark One

"So now we are working alone, right?" asked Segun.

"We are still investigating," replied Billy.

"What did you see up there, anyway?" asked Audrey.

"I don't know, can't tell," replied Billy as they enjoyed a glass of juice in Caput Amore. They had come to see the princess to ask for any form of help, even if just answers to their questions, but obviously it was hard being in Caput Amore, so they each had to blindfold themselves to avoid falling in love with any passersby.

"Okay, I still can't get used to this," said Segun.

"Used to what?" asked Audrey.

"The treatment. Like a random man just gave us fresh lemonade," replied Segun.

"Yes, and it's all free," said Billy. He wiped the beautiful tiny roses from his forehead that seemed to be dropping from the sky. "But we have to stay blindfolded or lose track of what we are here to find out." They reached the palace and met Princess Mabila.

"We are here to ask you about the Dark One. Tell us everything you know," said Billy.

"I thought you were here to thank me for giving you the crystal to handle your ghost problem," retorted Princess Mabila.

"I went up in the sky at Azrea and I saw the Dark One," said Billy.

"Aahhh?" the whole congregation gasped in shock.

"A boy, able to go up there?" said a court jester.

"I believe him," said the princess. "Follow me."

They followed the princess from the palace to the central library. That was where Billy was sent by Arthur Broadbottom a few weeks ago to break the chain, but Billy thought the chain was too beautiful to be broken. "Why are we here?" asked Audrey.

"This is the library. Everything we know about the Dark One is here," replied Princess Mabila. She used a key and opened the main door of the library. "So why is it always locked?" asked Segun.

"If we open it, people will read and learn about other things such as hate, jealousy and fear and they will not love any more. This is Caput Amore. We don't want such emotions to exist here," said the Princess.

"So why did Arthur Broadbottom want Billy to unlock the library?" asked Audrey.

"I don't know. They must think they are fixing everything.

Trying to make everywhere more like Earth, but that's only going to increase the influence of the Dark One. As you can see, we don't suffer from the Dark One here," replied Princess Mabila.

In the library, there was an entire section dedicated to the Dark One. "This is all the information that was gathered by my people hundreds of years ago on the Dark One," said the princess. "I'll come back and close the library in an hour." Billy picked up a book entitled 'The Conundrum of the Dark One'. Segun was looking at another book entitled 'The Dark One is God', while Audrey saw a book entitled 'Who is the Dark One'. Audrey read a large part of the book, skipping through chapters she found less relevant and reading entirely the chapters she found relevant. Segun, on the other hand had been looking at images while Billy almost swore he'd heard someone speaking to him inside the book he was reading.

"I think the dark one is a dragon," said Segun.

"They have photos of him in there?" asked Billy.

"Yes, they describe the Dark One as a bunch of things but many artists draw him as a dragon," responded Segun.

"I think it's female," said Audrey.

"The Dark One is a woman?" asked Billy.

"Yes, from the look of things," replied Audrey.

"I heard someone talking to me while I was reading the book I picked up from the book shelf—a woman," said Billy. Before long, the princess returned to lock the library, and they left Caput Amore.

* * *

Back at the Hidden Room, they had forgotten about the

crystal that stopped the ghosts from eavesdropping on their conversation. The ghosts realised that they were reading up on the Dark One and made an impromptu visit. "We heard you were researching about the Dark One," said Rabeus Farabus. "I am so proud of you guys," he said with a tear in his eye.

Verse 1

You have won the victory
Because you are my family
Hearing angels in the skies,
With victory in my hands,

Pre-Chorus
And I hold my bow steady as I go
Making sure that the arrow sees a sweet victory

Chorus
Wise and powerful
The walk with victory
For every victory
For every victory

Verse 2
If these fears step beside me,
I can stand up with victory
And more I wanna be, more
More bright and brighter

Pre-Chorus
Born of my soul to soar through the clouds,

To seek my victory, lord you have given me

Chorus
Wise and powerful
The walk with victory
For every victory
For every victory

Bridge
You can beat on her and you can beat on me
Put my loving cup into victory

Chorus
Wise and powerful
The walk with victory
For every victory
For every victory

"Volkodlakea is now beautiful as it once was. Indeed, the power of the Dark One is waning," said Viktor Ripmav who had just joined the singing.

"So now the Dark One only has a hold on Azrea?" asked Billy.

"Yes, but let us leave that alone," said Rabeus Farabus, but the teenagers weren't going to leave anything alone. They continued their investigations of the Dark One until one day, they went up to the highest mountain in the Kingdom of Azrea and discovered that there was an ancient observatory where some people had been observing the Dark One for hundreds of years. "So, it seems it's not only in Caput Amore that people have had an interest in the Dark One," said Audrey as they observed the ancient telescopes that were used to catch a glimpse of the Dark One. "Look, it's some kind of plane," said Audrey, pointing at a moderately sized octagonal vehicle.

"More like a spaceship," said Segun.

"Huh? So, someone went up there to see the Dark One?" asked Billy.

"Looks like they succeeded," commented Audrey.

"But they couldn't stop the Dark One—clearly," said Segun. Billy jumped inside the plane and started looking around. He sat on the pilot's chair pushed the start button but nothing happened. "It's not starting," he said with a sigh.

"That's not how to start it. Get out of there, you unsalted potato chip," said an old lady. She kept bumping into the furniture and old analog devices before she found her pair of glasses. "Let's see what we have here. It's three uninvited visitors," she went on.

"We are sorry, just looking around," apologised Audrey.

"Looking around for what, exactly? Out of there before you kill yourself," said the old lady. Billy struggled to get out of the pilot's chair but couldn't. "I can't seem to free myself from these belts," he yelled.

"Huh? Could you be the saviour?" gasped the old lady. Her eyes widened as she tried to make sense of the situation under the bright sun. The people of the Kingdom of Azrea had believed in a saviour for a very long time and she was no exception. "Well, if it suits you so perfectly, you must be here to save us from the Dark One."

"Actually, we are here to learn more about the Dark One," said Audrey.

"Is that so..." said the old lady. She looked through heaps of books piled on the floor and found a key inside a small green box. "This is the key. Be careful, O saviour."

Billy used the key to start the plane, and before long, he was up in the air. This time around, he was able to go higher up in the sky than he could when Alfred turned into a flying dragon. Using the radio, he communicated with the observatory. "This is Billy, over," he said.

"We can hear you. Do you see anything up there?" replied Segun and Audrey in unison. "No, nothing yet," replied Billy.

"Hang on, the Dark One should come soon," said the old lady. "I must hide now."

She went back into the room she came out of, but Segun wasn't going to take any chances. What if she turned into something so hideous? He thought. "Audrey, let's use this table to block the door to her room—give me a hand," he said.

Meanwhile, it had started getting darker as the Dark one approached, but still Billy couldn't get high enough. "This is Billy, can you guys hear me?" said Billy but there was no response. "Observatory, Observatory, is anyone there? Over." By then, Billy was beginning to come to terms with the matter — he was never going to see the Dark One. All he saw was a shadow and then he noticed a lone button on the dashboard with a capital letter 'O' on it. He wondered what that would do and without hesitation, he pressed the button and realised he was floating. He must have been in outer space, he thought. The button had launched the plane to the edge of space and then he saw the Dark One or the dark thing. It was so large that he could only see what seemed like a tail. It was a humongous dragon.

"Who is so puny but so daring enough to venture out into the dominion of masters?" said the Dark One. He was so large that everything vibrated when he spoke. "I am Billy. Are you the Dark One?"

"Haha, they call me that because my presence causes chain reactions," said the dragon.

"Why are you so evil? Because of you, people get hurt," said Billy.

"Hahaha, return to your world, child," responded the Dark One. Billy pushed a button to launch a missile at the Dark One. Maybe this could stop him, he thought. As the missile reached closer and closer to the Dark One who was already far away from Billy, the missile became too small for Billy to see it but it must have hit the target, because the Dark One turned around and came very close to Billy.

"Please, more, more of that delicious candy please," said the Dark One.

"Candy? That's a bomb to destroy you," replied Billy.

"To destroy me? Haha, I cannot be destroyed, child. I'm indestructible haha,"

"But the people who created this plane wanted to destroy you with it. Surely it is capable, right?" asked Billy.

"Haha, no, silly. They worship me across these worlds even though I never asked them to," responded the Dark One.

"What are you?" asked Billy.

"Haha. A long, long, long, long time ago. I was young like

you, Billy, and lived many a life across the worlds," said the Dark One.

"You know my name?"

"I know many things, my boy, and do not interrupt. One day I learnt the secret of travelling to the different worlds, just like you and your friends, but unfortunately for me I was alone and naïve. I got lost forever and very soon time and space mattered not. I wanted to know all about existence. How the worlds came to be," said the Dark One. He moved his large scaly tail and sent asteroids crashing into the Kingdom of Azrea. Billy thought 'how evil'. The Dark One then continued, "Very soon, I learnt that the worlds were created and maintained by the Archons. I tried to destroy the archons, so I travelled to their world," he paused and waved his fingers creating a cloudy illustration of his journey to the world of the archons and Billy's eyes glued to the illusion as the Dark One carried on with his story. The projection created by the Dark One against the darkness of outer space was so cinematic that Billy thought about his time at the cinema with Segun and Aunt Sarah. For a moment, he wondered if he'd ever see them again. In the projection, the Dark One is seen as a human visiting the world of the archons. The archons were like skyscrapers standing in an empty desert, holding each of the worlds in their hands. Billy saw Earth being held by an archon. He also saw Volkodlakea, Azrea and Caput Amore, also held by other archons. Billy noticed that there were other worlds too being held by other archons. Could this be true, or could it be some fake illusion created by the Dark One to deceive him? He wondered.

"How do I know all this is real?"

"Haha, if you don't believe me, you can go yourself," responded the Dark One.

"So you were human?"

"I had countless lives Billy, I've been animals, and humans alike," replied the Dark One.

"So, how did you become the Dark One?"

"Haha, I am not the Dark One. I am simply too powerful for the archons to put me into their little dream worlds like Earth. So, I move freely across the worlds in an indestructible body."

"But whenever you pass through Azrea, people turn into hideous creatures and destroy their homes."

"That is not my doing. When you breathe, Billy, microscopic organisms die all around you. You also enjoy your pork sausages, don't you?" replied the Dark One. "Let's say, I'll not pass through Azrea again then — if that will make you feel better."

"Do you remember your last life?" asked Billy.

"Very much so, my last few lives I was a female, but all short-lived."

Seventeen

Billy's Mother

Billy bid the Dark One goodbye and descended down through the clouds back to the hilltop observatory. Even though the Dark One had passed over the Kingdom of Azrea, it was not destroyed and the people had not turned into hideous creatures. They had Billy to thank for that; so, the king of Azrea held a festival to celebrate. Audrey and Segun were also happy to see the new changes in Azrea — it was now truly a fairytale land. "How did you defeat the Dark One, Billy?" asked Audrey.

"The Dark One has agreed not to pass over Azrea again," replied Billy.

"So he's not defeated?" asked Segun.

"Nah, not really," replied Billy.

* * *

Later that day, they returned to Earth and while at the Hidden Room, Billy couldn't wait to share his findings with the ghosts. He picked up the planchette and placed the hand of the ballerina inside the slot, and the room vibrated. Arthur Broadbottom appeared and said, "It has been long. Have you not travelled in a while?" They had been travelling but Segun had been using the crystal given to them by the princess, which stopped the ghost from knowing. "No, we have been travelling," replied Billy.

"Oh, is it?" Arthur Broadbottom asked a rhetorical question.

"Yes, I met the Dark One," replied Billy, and Arthur Broadbottom's ghostly face went whiter than ever. He cleared his throat and the other ghosts appeared.

"Billy, defeated the Dark One," he said and the other ghosts rejoiced.

"How did you defeat the Dark One?" asked Carla Reid.

"I simply spoke with him. He was a large Dragon. He agreed not to go to Azrea again," replied Billy.

"Hmm, that was very brave of you, Billy. Did he tell you anything else?"

"Yes, he told me about the archons," replied Billy.

"Oh, dangerous stuff," replied Carla Reid. Billy nodded in agreement and the ghost returned to their world.

* * *

It wasn't until after a few weeks had passed that Audrey became fascinated with the idea of visiting the world of the archons. She was so interested in what she might see, despite warnings from the ghosts not to go there. Mr Ade had had a dream in which he mentioned Raco. It was Aunt Sarah that had heard him in his sleep during the night. "You said you were in the world of the sprites. So, the last time you wanted to drink sprite and last night you were in sprite world with a person called Raco and you called her mother. Are you okay?"

"Oh, just a dream, dear, you know," replied Mr Ade. Segun overheard their conversation as he got ready for school and thought that was strange. He mentioned it to Audrey, which only fuelled her interest in the world of the archons. That evening, they travelled to Caput Amore looking for Raco, but being a traveller like them, there was no telling where she could be at any given time. The princess of Caput Amore reckoned Raco could be found on Earth — So they journeyed back together. While back on Earth, Audrey, Segun, and Princess Mabila found Billy in the basement. He had found a rolled up paper with the instructions for making a plane which could reach the Dark One.

"These are the instructions for making a plane, like the one in Azrea," said Billy.

"But this was never made. They need a special type of metal which is only found in Azrea," said Princess Mabila.

"I think your mother was trying to make a plane like that," said Audrey.

"Let's ask her," said Segun.

"Later," said Billy. He moved a couple more old boxes and found a diary with the initials 'C', 'R'. "This was my mum's diary," he said. Looking through the diary, he saw a note which read in part '*... find me in Azrea, we can destroy the Dark One.*' It was signed by Raco.

"Now we are getting somewhere," said Audrey. They quickly went up to the Hidden Room and picked up the Book of Doors, but they couldn't find anything about the world of the archons. Billy did what he usually did, and his mother, Carla Reid, appeared. "Were you trying to create a plane to get to the Dark One?" asked Billy. Carla Reid hesitated to answer, her eyes looking worrisome. She finally said, "Yes, I was," but the words were almost mumbled. "I never made it," she added.

"I found your diary," said Billy. "Why didn't you tell us you knew Raco?"

"We just wanted you to concentrate on fixing the realms, Billy. Remember the ghosts problems? People were seeing ghosts everywhere on Earth? People were being stuck in the interim world and not moving on to their next lives? That was the most important thing. Let's deal with the Dark One later," she replied, fading away into the background shortly after.

Princess Mabila wanted to see the plane that was at the observatory in Azrea, so the four of them travelled to Azrea. They looked everywhere for the plane, but it was missing. Instead, they found Raco in the king's courtyard. "Do you know Mr Ade?" asked Billy.

"Yes, he's my friend. A mind of a warrior he has. He does great works across the worlds," replied Raco.

"But he's my father and knows nothing about the worlds," said Billy.

"Oh, don't be silly, of course he does," said Raco.

"No, he doesn't," said Segun, "trust me."

"Then how does he come here every now and then and perform miraculous feats?" asked Raco.

"I've seen him in Takrea — Earth—. He only travels when sleeping," Princess Mabila chimed in, confirming what Billy and Segun were saying.

"Interesting, not a conscious traveller—remarkable," said Raco. She left the courtyard and headed toward a small room where she laid down. "Are you here for the plane?" she asked.

"Yes, we are," replied Billy.

"I can't let you have it," she said. "The Dark One is a sacred being and you mustn't see it again. The Dark One is God."

"No, he's not. So Arthur Broadbottom was right. You are working for the Dark One!" yelled Billy.

"Seize them," she said and tiny leprechauns surrounded the doors, but Billy was able to use his ring, which beamed them away from the King's Palace, placing them near the exit of Azrea.

"Do you have the Book of Doors with you?" asked Princess Mabila. "Yes, it's in my bag," replied Audrey.

"Okay, let's see," said the Princess. She opened the missing pages and cast a spell to reveal the pages but nothing happened. "We've already tried that," said Audrey.

"I have an idea," said Segun.

"Yeah, what is it?" asked Princess Mabila.

"Clearly, the ghosts in the Reid House are not being honest with us. They didn't write the Book of Doors," said Segun. He stretched his arms and yawned. "If we can find out who really wrote it, they can tell us what's in the missing pages," he added.

"How in the world are we supposed to do that?" fumed Audrey.

"Wait, he might have a point. My dad—Mr Ade— said it was a board game. Turn it over," said Billy. Audrey flipped over the Book of Doors and there was a scribble on the back page which said 'identify the lords of the book to find pages on hidden doors, hidden worlds, and hidden treasures'. "No one could have written this book but elves," said Princess Mabila.

"Elves?" said Audrey. "In that case we have to go to the world of the sprites."

* * *

The world of the sprites was difficult to find, but with the help of the princess, they eventually found an entrance in Caput Amore. The sprites were as they were the last time the teenagers had encountered them — seemingly mindless and preoccupied with their chores. So it was an uphill task locating the 'lord' of the book—he could be any sprite. Instead, Billy suggested they go to the library and find a psychic copy of the Book of Doors.

"Brilliant, Billy. This is it," said Princess Mabila as she picked up the Book of Doors from an old forgotten shelf. Audrey got closer to see all the pages she'd wanted to see but couldn't for a very long time. The princess flipped through and discovered countless missing pages, including where to find baby dragons, how to build around doors and use a building as a point of interdimensional travel, and unknown or lost technologies, but nothing about the world of the archons. "You can't find that in there," said a sprite. Princess Mabila gasped as the sprite made his presence known. He came nearer and said, "What are you doing touching my memory?"

"Oh sorry, we have the original one but some pages are missing," replied Audrey. "Hmm, clever, but I myself was not able to find the world of the archons, for it is not a world," replied the sprite.

"Let's just forget it and go back home," said Segun.

"No, we've already come this far," said Billy. The sprite stopped flapping his dragonfly-like wings and sat down on a bench next to Audrey and Princess Mabila. He sighed and said, "I left Volkodlakea when the wars with the humans and vampires started. I went to Earth where I wrote this book. I had tremendous help from a very interesting lady called Carla Reid. I'm sure she can help."

"That's my mum. She's dead, but we can still see her," said Billy.

"She is dead in your world but present and living her next life, in Caput Amore. I must go now and continue to purge myself of my previous mistakes," said the sprite, he flapped his wings and flew away toward the pillar of light at the centre of the world of the sprites, leaving the four of them in the darkened old library.

"Okay, guys, that was super weird. Your mom is a ghost, and she's also alive in Caput Amore?" said Audrey.

"I know who it is. It must be Raco," said Billy, his facial expression blank.

"It doesn't take a genius to come to the same conclusion," said Princess Mabila.

* * *

Raco at the Kingdom of Azrea

Moments later, they returned to the Kingdom of Azrea and caught up with Raco who apologised for her earlier behavior. "It has been my life's goal to defeat the Dark One. I built the plane, but I'm scared of flying. When I learnt you used the plane but made deals with the Dark One, I was absolutely livid. The missile would have destroyed him. You can't make deals with such a villain," she said. Billy nodded to acknowledge his mistake, but deep down, he knew it wasn't a mistake. He knew he'd been lucky the Dark One did not harm him. "I did fire the missile, but he just swallowed it," responded Billy.

Raco shook her head in disbelief. "Why are you here?" she asked.

"Can you help us go to the world of the Archons?" asked Billy.

"Oh, that's a myth, haha," she laughed.

"You are my mother," said Billy, seeing her face changing from slightly jovial to a hysteric confusion he added "in a past life."

"I don't believe in past lives," she replied.

"Just lie down here already," yelled Princess Mabila. She drew her dagger and pointed it at Raco, who agreed to lie down on her resting couch. "I will perform a past life regression," said Princess Mabila. The princess projected the images from Raco's mind on the wall, which showed Carla Reid on Earth while she was alive and her efforts toward creating the plane. She never succeeded in creating it, but finally created the plane in her new life as Raco.

"Where is the world of the Archons?" asked Princess Mabila and the projection showed the Dark One near a gate. This frightened Raco and she snapped out of the trance with a start. "Where am I?" she screamed in fright.

"Relax, you are here in Azrea," responded Princess Mabila.

"So now we know the Dark One knows the entrance. Billy, you'll have to talk to him," said Audrey.

"Yeah, I know," replied Billy. He went up in the plane to the edge of space, waited where he expected the Dark One to pass.

Eighteen

The World of the Archons

High above the Kingdom of Azrea billy waited and waited for the Dark One to pass but he never did. The Dark One had honoured his part of the promise and never passed over the Kingdom of Azrea, ever again. Instead, it was in Limuria that they finally caught up with the Dark One.

"We are travellers from Earth looking for the Dark One," said Billy as they entered an old disused solar temple in Limuria. "Welcome, the Dark One can be reached through prayers. We are trying to bring back the sun to Limuria," responded a member of the resistance, who was part of a cult. Billy glanced at Audrey and Segun and sighed. All their work was being undone, he thought, but he didn't care about what the ghosts wanted anymore. They now had their own mission, and it was simply just to see the world of the archons. "How do we pray?" Billy reluctantly asked. "Just kneel here and do as the others are doing," directed the member of the resistance. He pointed at a small crowd behind a door that was praying to the Dark One. Audrey and Segun began to pray as the others were doing, but Billy hesitated before joining in. However, when he prayed something miraculous happened—the Dark One listened. There was a statue of a man with wings at the centre of the room, which represented the Dark One. As Billy prayed, the statue's eyes came to life and pupils appeared. He spoke — "We meet again, young one."

"Dark One, please tell me how to get to the world of the archons."

"Haha, you are looking in the wrong places. The world of the archons can only be reached from Earth—remember, we have all done it before," said the Dark One before vanishing into nothingness and the cold eyes of the statue becoming lifeless again. That was so brief and confusing, thought Billy. He tried praying to the Dark One again, but nothing happened.

***

They returned to the Hidden Room and Audrey spent at least an hour going through the Book of Doors for the umpteenth time, but she could not find anything useful. "So there must be a way to reach the world from the Hidden Room," she said. Billy wondered how she came to that conclusion.

"Yes, remember that world where the souls are? Maybe it's there" commented Segun.

"No, it isn't," replied Billy. "I'm calling the ghosts," he added dismissively. He picked up the planchette and placed the hand of the ballerina inside the slot, and the ghosts appeared one by one. "Mr Broadbottom, are there other worlds we can reach from here?" asked Billy.

"Yes, there must be, but I have never seen it done myself. Only the four doors lead to the four primary worlds," responded Arthur Broadbottom.

"There is another way," said Carla Reid, "but it is risky. I am afraid only Billy can go on this journey," she added.

"Why?" asked Audrey.

"Because the other worlds are too dissimilar from Earth. If you go there, you will forget that you are from Earth. It is only possible to go there in dreams," replied Arthur Broadbottom.

"Where are the photos you took on your phone, Segun?" asked Audrey. Apparently, Segun had taken the photos of the missing pages from the Book of Doors they'd seen in the world of the sprites. "Right here," replied Segun. Audrey went through the pages and found exactly what she was looking for. The Reid House itself could be used as a travelling craft. She showed Billy a page that had pictures and his face turned from a slight frown of disappointment to the look of instant gratification.

"Ahh, so that's how it's done," said Billy. He placed the hand of the ballerina in a slot in the wall behind a cabinet in the Hidden Room. Around the slot was written 'the world of archons', but nothing happened. "Everybody hold hands and let us repeat the process," said Arthur Braodbottom as he fixed his bowtie. Shortly after, the room darkened, and they looked out the window, noticing the earthly surroundings slowly disappearing. The garden was gone and the trees. Soon to be replaced by an alien world with strange colours. "Okay, nobody leaves this house. It's for your own safety," said Viktor Ripmav.

"I have a question, you told us you wrote the Book of Doors but we met the actual writer—an elf in the world of sprites who said he wrote it?" asked Audrey but the ghosts did not reply, they had no answer. Instead, they looked dumbfounded.

"Also, if you are Carla Reid, how come you are a ghost and you are also Raco?" asked Segun. He had been itching to ask that question.

"I admit, the book might have been slightly plagiarised but I assure you, we wrote the Book of Doors," replied Arthur Broadbottom. At which point Rabeus Farabus and Viktor Ripmav were as quiet as the world outside that was gradually furnishing itself with alien objects. Billy opened the door to the Hidden Room and a strange light flowed in. "It's weird, but I'm beginning to like this world," gushed Audrey.

"Wow, the whole house has been transported," said Segun.

"Look, there is something near the door. Close it Billy?" yelled Audrey.

"Relax, it's not something. It's someone. It is I, Alfred, a man again," he answered. He peered into the Hidden Room and motioned for the three of them to follow him. They sighed in relief. "Where are we going?" asked Billy.

"For all the time I'd spent being a dog, I've gathered so much information about this place, but just couldn't speak about it," responded Alfred. They followed Alfred downstairs and saw Mr Ade lying on the Sofa. "What if he wakes up?" asked Segun. "Don't worry, they are dreaming now. They can't remember any of this," replied Alfred.

"This is exactly what the Dark One described," said Billy. He opened the front door and went out into the world of the archons and, just as the Dark One had said, there were huge pillars holding each of the worlds. "The worlds are illusions created by the archons. We are trapped in this cycle of life, death, and rebirth. Only the Dark One had freed himself," commented Alfred as he stood right next to the main door of the Reid House, looking out into the world of the archons, but he dared not step outside.

"And that is why he is able to travel freely through one illusion after another. He is outside the worlds," concluded Audrey.

"That's dope," said Segun, "you knew about this?" He asked Arthur Broadbottom. The ghost looked paler than usual. "No, not at all. I must say, I myself, I'm dismayed," replied Arthur Broadbottom.

"But, let us get to the bottom of this, together," said Rabeus Farabus.

"How?" asked Segun.

"Well, it will take time, young man, but for now. We have seen the world of the archons and we must return as soon as possible," responded Rabeus Farabus but Audrey was nowhere in sight. She had wandered outside the Reid House; their only protection.

"Audrey!" yelled Segun but his voice only returned echoes bouncing off of dust floating in expansive space. The world of the archons was indescribable, full of strange objects suspended in the air. There was no sense of up or down and no cardinal directions. The only thing that reminded them of themselves was the presence of the Reid House, hanging in the middle of an alien reality. Segun thought it would be a good idea to search for Audrey around the perimeter of the house to avoid going too far into the world of the archons and so did Arthur Broadbottom, Viktor Ripmav and Carla Reid. However, Billy and Alfred went a little bit farther into the world and Rabeus Farabus followed them. "Billy, don't go too far," screamed Rabeus Farabus but the faster he ran toward Billy and Alfred the farther away he got from them. "We are over here," replied Billy. He turned around and noticed Rebeaus Farabus had turned into a stone pillar. "Huh, Alfred, look! What happened to Rabeus Farabus?"

"If you don't have a soul, you cannot exist here. The only explanation is that Rabeus Farabus was never human," responded Alfred.

"Let's help him," yelled Billy.

"No, I came here to find a new world. I am tired of being a dog. You must find your friend and go back home," replied Alfred as he continued to walk farther and deeper into the strange world. "We can help you find a world, Alfred. You don't have to do it this way." Billy tried to stop Alfred, but it fell on deaf ears. He turned around and saw Rabeus Farabus stuck to an object. "You can't help me anymore. Go and find Audrey," yelled Rabeus Farabus. It was the last words he uttered before completely turning into a solid pillar.

***

Billy ran back to the Reid House and met Segun still searching around the house while keeping his hand on the walls of the house and repeating the words, "I am Segun, I am from Earth," but still it helped little, as he couldn't recognise Billy. "Segun, it's me Billy!"

"No, it's me Segun, I am from Earth," responded Segun — his face blank.

"What is wrong? Where are the rest of the ghosts?"

"I am from Earth, I am Segun, it will not affect me. I am going home, I am S... Segun," he stammered and carried on, going around the house. "Let's get you back in," said Billy. He shoved Segun back into the house from the kitchen door and Segun fell like a plate, right on his face and still continued repeating his mantra. Billy realised that Carla Reid, Viktor Ripmav and Arthur Broadbottom had also turned into lifeless pillars. Could that be what happened to Audrey? But she is human, so it couldn't have happened to her, he thought.

Not too far from the Reid House, Billy heard someone breathing heavily. He walked toward the sound. "Billy, I couldn't leave this little spot." it was Audrey. Billy was glad to see her and motioned for her to follow him, but she still couldn't. Upon close examination, he realised that she'd turned into a pillar just like Rabeus Farabus. Tried as he had to bring Audrey back to life, he couldn't. He remembered Carla Reid's warning and wished they'd all listened. He began to feel a slight irritation on the skin of his ears. He placed his finger behind his ear lobes and it was moist from bleeding. The world had become so irritating that he couldn't even understand what he was feeling. His inner t-shirt was stained with blood and his feet and fingers were hurting so much, followed by his knees and elbows. He tried to use his ring, maybe it could teleport him back to the Hidden Room, maybe the house was still there, which he could not see anymore. Maybe he just couldn't find it, he thought, but the powers of the ring were muted in the strange world of the archons. Time was running out. Billy reached an upside down hill and began to climb it, which then became right side up. The world was indeed weird, he thought.By then he settled in his new fate. Maybe he was never going to go home, but what about his friend Audrey?

He's got to help her get home. At least Segun was home. "Alfred, where are you?" shouted Billy. It took a while before he heard Alfred's reply.

"Over here, over here," Alfred's voice echoed.

"I'm coming toward you. Keep talking," replied Billy. He trekked and trekked as Alfred kept speaking. Finally, Billy reached a point on the hill which had a small lake suspended in the air and a crater below. Billy ran down toward the centre of the crater and saw Alfred whimpering. He had been turned into a dog again. "Billy, we can't escape this world of the archons. Only you can go back home, but you will also succumb to the strange physics of this world if you don't become stronger. Change your body, Billy!" said Alfred before he crystallised into solid rock.

****

Billy wandered on and on, thinking about what Alfred said. He recalled that Alfred had once turned into a dragon in the kingdom of Azrea. He thought of himself as a dragon and slowly; he grew scales all over his body and the pain of being in the world of the archons became tolerable. Billy could now move a lot faster. So he flew up to one of the archons that was creating the illusion of Earth and he tried to enter the world of Earth from there, but he was struck by a white light. At that moment, before Billy crashed to the ground, he recalled the perfectly impervious body of the Dark One and he transformed himself into a Dragon just like the Dark One and in doing so; he avoided crashing. The ground simply gave way to his enormous and powerful body. So this is how the Dark One passes from world to world, thought Billy. He flew toward the archon that was creating the illusion of Earth one more time and he was struck by the thunderous white light again, but he couldn't feel anything. Billy flew into Earth and he could see himself floating over his school and all the places he used to know. He visited other worlds, too, which he was never able to visit without the body of the Dark One. It was so liberating and beautiful that Billy began to forget who he was. He was no longer Billy; he was the Dark One. Moving from world to world was so joyous, he thought.

"Snap out of it, Billy. Are you okay?" asked Audrey as she snapped her finger across Billy's dazed face. "Huh?" gasped Billy. "Audrey, are you okay?"

"Yes, of course I'm okay," responded Audrey. Billy looked across the Hidden Room and saw Segun seated on the couch and Alfred barking outside the door, trying to get in, while Billy's hand was holding the hand of the ballerina about to insert it in the little slot on the wall of the Hidden Room.

"Billy, from the looks of things, you've been shown a future so undesirable," said Arthur Broadbottom. He was as alive as ever as a ghost, along with all the others. "Yes, I have. I think we should forget about the world of the archons," replied Billy.

END

Hamza Lawal's first book, Legend of the Huskahs was a global success. It sold thousands of copies and now he is venturing into the realms of fantasy with this new book. You can find more about his work at fictionhamza.com.